STAGE TO CHEYENNE

When Malloy rode into Masonville on his long journey north, he found a town struggling to survive. The Wyoming cattle barons aimed to regain the old open range and their hired gunfighters were ready to kill anyone who stood in their way. Only a regular stagecoach to Cheyenne offered a chance of peace. Malloy's hard fists and ready guns had been hired elsewhere, but when the townsfolk called on him for help, Malloy could not turn aside. Masonville offered him a chance to start his life over – if only his Peacemaker could keep him alive!

STAGE TO CHEYENNE

STAGE TO CHEYENNE

by

Jack Edwardes

Dales Large Print Books
Long Preston, North Yorkshire,
BD23 4ND, England.

British Library Cataloguing in Publication Data.

Stage to Cheyenne
    Edwardes, Jack.

    A catalogue record of this book is
    available from the British Library

    ISBN   1-84262-388-5 pbk

First published in Great Britain 2004 by Robert Hale Limited

Published in Large Print 2005 by arrangement with
Robert Hale Limited

Dales Large Print is an imprint of Library Magna Books Ltd.

Printed and bound in Great Britain by
T.J. (International) Ltd., Cornwall, PL28 8RW

CHAPTER ONE

Malloy was saddling up for the day when he saw the riders maybe half a mile to the west. He looked around quickly but he was well hidden. From the shelter of the cotton-woods he could see the three figures out-lined against the bunch and buffalo grass. One rider was maybe a couple of yards ahead of the two others.

Malloy pulled steadily on his mount's girth, threading the latigo through the rigging ring before tying the final knot. Shifting to grasp the horn with one hand, the cantle with the other, he pulled strongly, checking the saddle was secure. Then he pulled up the flap of his saddle-bag.

'Best take a look,' he said aloud to the palomino.

Groping inside his war bag, he pushed aside a leather sack of pemmican, and pulled out his spyglass. He moved through the trees, taking care to remain hidden, and looked down from his high point. With the morning sun behind him there was no risk of the spyglass giving away his presence. He raised it to his eye, bringing the three riders into focus with a twist of the barrel. Rangemen, he guessed at first, seeing their rough trail clothes and scrubby mounts. Then, as the men drew closer, he wasn't so sure. He saw that the leading rider, his face obscured by a slouch hat, favoured a left-hand draw, his long-barrelled sidearm tied down with a leather thong.

'A lotta iron for a cowhand,' Malloy muttered aloud.

The other two riders wore California spurs, unlike the smaller Plains spurs favoured by Malloy. One of the two men at the rear was head and shoulders above his fellow riders, his hat with its rounded high crown making him appear even taller. But he was no Indian. Malloy could see the pale hair falling to his shoulders.

Malloy lowered the spyglass and glanced behind him, checking his palomino was settled. No point in taking chances. He'd heard talk of trouble in these parts. On the trail to the south he'd met a bunch of homesteaders looking for a new place to settle after throwing in their hands around here. He was maybe only ten miles from Masonville. The local law should reach this far but it could still be dangerous to come across strangers.

Then he smiled briefly, fine lines around his eyes creasing his weathered face. Ruefully, he kicked at the base of the tree-trunk. Maybe the weeks on the trail were getting to him. Folks would start thinking him some pilgrim ready to jump at his own shadow. Most likely the three riders were about their honest business. The leader's Navy Colt, if that's what it was, could have been gotten from anywhere. Maybe won in a poker game. There was no law against wearing fancy spurs with big rowels. Yet there was something about the three riders that made him pause. How many range-men had he seen carrying that amount of iron? None of the men wore a badge on his vest. Some deep instinct overrode Malloy's doubts, urging him to be wary.

The spyglass held loosely down by his side, Malloy leaned against the bark of the cottonwood. He'd wait to roll himself a smoke. He had enough Bull Durham in its muslin sack to last until Masonville. When the riders had passed he'd make his way into town. A hot tub, a visit to the barbershop, and a clean bunk would set him right. There was bound to be a Chinaman's place in town. Decent grub would make a welcome change from the jerky he'd been eating on the trail. A couple of days to rest up, then he'd be riding north again. Another month and he'd be throwing off his trail clothes.

Suddenly, he pushed himself off the cottonwood to stand with his eyes fixed on the three riders. The leader had turned his mount, heading for the stand of pines that bordered a small creek on the other side of the trail. The two other riders remained close behind him. Only half-hidden among the thinly spread pines, the men and horses remained in Malloy's view as they passed between the trees.

Were they only intent on watering their mounts? Malloy knew the water in the creek was good. The palomino and he had filled their bellies the previous evening before taking to the higher ground. Yet none of the riders moved his horse to the water. Instead, they bunched close. Again Malloy looked back at his palomino, but the animal was quietly nibbling at the grass. The wind was in the wrong direction for the strangers' horses to pick up its scent.

Bringing his spyglass up to his eye again Malloy saw the rider in the slouch hat dismount and reach into his saddle-bag. There was a glint of metal from a spyglass similar to Malloy's own. He stepped back quickly, shielding his body with the trunk of the cottonwood. But none of the men turned his face in Malloy's direction, the two riders watching the dismounted man scramble up the sloping ground between the pines. Malloy saw him throw himself to the ground at the top of the slope and bring the brass barrel of his spyglass to bear on the trail.

From his vantage point, Malloy looked southwards beyond the man across the broad sweep of the open range. Nothing moved. Malloy remained still, the spyglass to his eye, waiting to see what the riders were expecting. Several minutes later, after lowering his spyglass twice to rest his eye, he saw the dust cloud along the trail. His fingers curled tightly around the metal. Was he seeing a bunch of riders? Or was it a wagon? Then as the trail bent, the rays of the morning sun fell ahead of the dust cloud and he could see more clearly. Stagecoach! Malloy breathed in deeply as he lowered his spyglass.

'You're jumpier than a jack-rabbit,' he muttered to himself.

Then he stood still, looking hard down at the men. As the look-out scrambled back down towards his horse, Malloy saw the other two riders lean forward to draw their long-guns from the scabbards on their saddles. Throwing himself on his horse, the look-out drew his sidearm.

Malloy swore softly. He'd been weeks on the trail from Texas and until now he'd managed to stay out of trouble. Now he found himself in this barrel of tar. The stage must be carrying something valuable. Silver, Malloy guessed. He'd heard there was a mine around these parts. The three riders sure as hell weren't going to be riding point on the stage.

Again Malloy swore softly. Why should he care? Nobody in these parts would give two bits if he ended up with his face in the dirt. Another month's riding, and he'd take the job he'd been offered. A damn good job that would give him fine clothes and decent whiskey. A regular place of his own. No Mexican rustlers hell-bent on shooting him down. He could just stand here and watch the action. Malloy breathed in deeply. A moment later a smile flickered across his face. What the hell! Maybe there'd be a reward, and some travelling money would come in handy.

He looked around. The *bandidos* had

picked their spot. As the trail bent between the higher grounds either side of the trail, they'd be hidden until the stage was abreast of the pines. Malloy looked south again. The outline of the stagecoach was now clearer among the dust thrown up from its wheels and the hoofs of its trotting horses. Malloy snapped his spyglass shut and checked the ground ahead of him down to the trail.

He spun on his heel and moved through the cotton-woods to shove away his spyglass. He unhitched his reins from a sapling and mounted the palomino.

'Damned glad you're clear-footed,' he said softly, tugging gently at the animal's ear. 'Reckon you're gonna be smellin' gunsmoke again mighty soon.'

With a touch of his heels to the palomino's flanks, Malloy moved forward, head bent to avoid the low branches. Nearing the edge of the stand of trees, he heard the cries from the driver of the stage ringing out across the open country. He could see the stage clearly now. Two men sat high above the horses. The driver was a short man bulked out in a woodsman's mackinaw. Alongside him on the box sat the messenger in a dark slicker, a shotgun resting easily across his knees. As the stage followed the twist of the trail,

Malloy caught sight of a green splash of colour inside the stage. A woman's dress, he guessed. He drew his Winchester from its scabbard alongside his right leg. He hoped the woman was smart enough to keep low and not scream too much when the shooting started.

Malloy dallied his reins around the horn while watching the stage reach the last bend before the pine trees. For a moment it disappeared from view then reappeared twenty yards short of where the riders were hidden. None of the men moved. They sat taut in their saddles, their weapons at the ready. Malloy guessed they planned to let the stage pass them.

If the driver and his messenger were aware of the danger they gave no indication. As the thought came to Malloy the three riders broke from cover twenty yards behind the stage. All now had bandannas pulled up over their faces. Each man rode his mount with one hand clutching his reins. The leading rider held his sidearm high. The others held long-guns.

At first, neither of the men on the stage looked back, the sounds of the three riders maybe lost below the creaking of the stage and the drumming of the hoofs of their own six horses. But as the *bandidos* drew closer, the messenger suddenly moved, half-crouching on the swaying stage as he swung his shotgun to blast in their direction. His aim must have been off target. Two shots rang out from the long-guns.

Malloy saw the messenger clutch at his shoulder and fall back, the shotgun falling from his grasp to bounce along the dirt of the trail. The driver grasped his side as if hit, but he remained in control of his team, hauling on the lines, slowing the stage.

Malloy sucked in air. 'Time to go!'

He kicked into the flanks of his palomino, and burst out from the shelter of the cottonwoods, the clear air ringing with a yell that erupted from his expanded lungs. The palomino charged sure-footedly down the slope. Malloy raised his Winchester, sighting along the barrel.

The vicelike grip of his thighs kept Malloy steady in the saddle. His finger curled and squeezed, and the *bandido* with the raised sidearm was jerked from his saddle as if clutched by an invisible hand. Brass spun through the air as Malloy levered his Winchester.

The palomino swung to the right for a few strides before swinging back to the left. The

15

slug from a long-gun whipped through the air past Malloy, the sound reaching him an instant later. He swung his Winchester around as the second *bandido*'s horse reared, forelegs pawing at the air. There was the smack of Malloy's bullet striking horseflesh. A high animal scream rent the air and the horse toppled to the ground, flinging its rider into the dirt.

Again Malloy swung his Winchester around but the third *bandido*, his tall hat bent low over his saddle, had turned his mount. The palomino hit the dirt of the trail at the bottom of the slope, shifting Malloy's aim a fraction. Then the fleeing rider was lost to sight around the bend in the trail, the beat of his horse's hoofs fading rapidly.

Breathing heavily, white lines around his nose showing the stress of the encounter, Malloy urged his palomino forward until he reached the two men on the ground. One lay face down, his hat half-off, soaked in a pool of blood. The back of his head showed he wouldn't be getting up. The other, thrown from the dead horse, lay on his back, his eyes wide with fear, his face twitching uncontrollably. Malloy thrust his Winchester into its scabbard and drew his Peacemaker.

'Don't do that!' A high feminine voice cut through the air.

Malloy looked around at the stage, which had halted ten yards away, steam rising from the flanks of the panting horses. On the ground beside the open door stood a young fair-haired woman. Below her fancy hat, her face was pale. A thin film of dust dulled the green silk of her dress. Malloy remembered then that he hadn't heard her scream. Maybe she was tougher than she looked.

His breathing had slackened and the tension was draining from his muscles.

'I don't plan on killin' him in cold blood, if that's what you're thinking, ma'am,' he said.

Paying her no further attention, Malloy slipped from his saddle, to stand looking down on the man. 'But I might just have to.'

'I ain't aimin' to make trouble, mister.'

Malloy reached down and took the man's sidearm. 'You stay on the ground 'til I'm ready for you. Move an' I'll kill you.'

'Sure, mister. Sure.' His face continued to twitch violently.

Malloy looked up again to speak to the young woman but she'd turned her back, helping an older man wearing a city suit and a derby hat who must have been inside the stage. Together the pair reached up to help the messenger to the ground. The older man half-turned as Malloy approached them, leading his horse.

'Samuel L. Stockin, sir. We are in your debt.'

'You want me to take a look at that?' Malloy asked the messenger.

The messenger, ashen-faced, grunted with pain as he was helped down to the ground. He shook his head.

'Got lucky, I guess. Just winged me. Doc'll see to it. Kinda like my shotgun back, though.'

The young woman turned to Malloy. 'We owe you our lives Mr...?'

'Malloy, ma'am.'

'Then if you can find Charlie's shotgun, we'll get him into the stage and take care of him.'

Malloy nodded. For a woman who'd been shot at only a few minutes before, she sure knew how to give orders. Maybe she was used to getting her way with those sky-blue eyes and that soft pale skin. He glanced around at the man on the ground, but he was still, his eyes screwed shut.

Malloy looked up at the driver. 'You OK?'

The driver sat staring ahead, his six lines in

one gnarled hand, the other rubbing at his side. He turned his head away for a moment to eject a stream of black tobacco juice on to the trail. Discoloured teeth showed in his mouth when he turned back to Malloy. He reached beneath his mackinaw and held up a battered piece of metal.

'Guess it's my lucky day. Felt the slug go past. Broke my danged timepiece. Like bein' kicked by a mule.' He thrust the misshapen metal into his mackinaw pocket. A wide grin split his lined face. 'Mighty grateful to you, Mr Malloy.'

'You carryin' silver?' Malloy said. The woman shot him a sharp backward glance as she stepped up to the coach after Stockin and the messenger.

'I ain't carryin' nothin',' the driver said. 'An' that goes for the passengers as well. God's honest truth.'

Malloy frowned. 'Those *bandidos* aimin' to kill someone?'

'I ain't sure.' The driver released another stream of tobacco juice. 'But this here stage ain't worth much.'

Malloy's expression didn't alter. 'I'll get Charlie his shotgun an' ride into town with you,' he said. 'The sheriff can take care of this road agent.'

The driver nodded in the direction of the creek. The dead man's horse stood quietly by the water, its head down, nibbling at the grass.

'I guess the buzzard-bait'll carry two, if you've a mind to bring in that dead critter.'

The driver flicked at the six horses with his lines. The two leaders walked forward, and the stage moved ahead. As the horses drew away Malloy saw that the driver was right about the stage. Bare wood showed through peeling paint. Leather straps were rubbed through and beginning to break up. One of the wheels showed a fine crack.

So what were the *bandidos* after? If they'd been fixing to kill the messenger or the driver they'd have bushwhacked the stage when passengers weren't around. The stage was ready for kindling wood, and nobody was carrying anything worth stealing. Or so he'd been told. And why were there only two passengers? The cash they'd paid to travel would barely cover the horse feed. Something was going on here he hadn't yet got a handle on.

CHAPTER TWO

The stagecoach had left the trail and was twenty yards down Masonville's Main Street when the townsfolk began to gather. Men in working clothes beneath dusty aprons stood alongside women in plain cotton dresses that swept the boardwalks. Several men wore city clothes. Three Shoshones stood together watching with brown-marbled eyes. In front of a dry-goods store two women showed high-button shoes beneath the hems of silk dresses. After weeks alone on the trail their high-pitched voices sounded odd in Malloy's ears. The women's voices became shriller as Malloy rode into their view twenty yards behind the stage.

Then a wave of noise surged along the boardwalk as the townsfolk saw the body across the horse being ridden by Malloy's prisoner. One or two of the men shouted out questions. Malloy ignored them. They'd get their answers soon enough from the people on board the stage.

He glanced around as he rode down Main

Street. Masonville looked as if it had once been prosperous but was now finding the going hard. Freshly painted stores were flanked by storefronts that had seen better days. A few men hung around gazing at his progress as if they had little else to do. A couple of storefronts were boarded up as if abandoned by their owners.

Half-way down the street, the stage driver turned around and called out:

'Fifty yards past the saloon, Mr Malloy. Sheriff Campbell.'

Malloy lifted a hand in acknowledgement. He saw a crowd begin to surround the stage as it halted near a sign pointing to the town's livery. The clear voice of the fair-haired woman and the deeper tones of Stockin cut through the excited chatter as a path was cleared for the wounded messenger.

'Keep ridin',' Malloy called to his prisoner. He turned to the half a dozen townsfolk gathering alongside him. 'OK, folks, stage driver'll tell you all you need to know.'

Scenting a more ready source of news, they turned away, save for a couple of small boys in knee-length britches and rough boots. Backing away across the street, their eyes fixed on the dead man, they climbed the steps to skitter along the boardwalk keeping pace with Malloy as he made his way towards the sheriff's office.

The word of his arrival must have spread fast. By the time he was level with the saloon half a dozen men stood in front of the batwing doors. One of them held a beer glass in his hands. Malloy tasted the dust on his lips. When he'd finished with the sheriff he'd make for the saloon. Masonville, he reckoned, owed him a couple of beers.

Two men with stars on their leather vests stood waiting below a painted sign announcing the sheriff's office. The younger man, a deputy, stepped down to the dirt of the street as Malloy's prisoner reached the hitching-rail. The deputy reached up and heaved the man from his horse, the prisoner making no effort to resist as he was dragged to the dirt of the street, his head bowed.

'Seein' as you ain't got a sidearm, Caleb Wood, an' this here stranger behind you has that cannon on his hip, I reckon you ain't gonna be threatenin' decent folks any more,' the deputy said. He stepped forward and turned the dead man's head so as to see his face.

'An' neither is your old pard Colorado, I guess.'

Malloy slid easily from his saddle.

'Three of 'em attacked the stage. One got away.'

The sheriff moved forward on the board-walk. A Marshal Colt was on his hip. He was tall, carrying the weight around his belt of a man who liked his food. Above the bushy moustaches his face was etched with deep lines.

'Throw Wood in the cage,' he ordered his deputy. 'Then take that Colorado critter over to Sam Johnson. The town'll have to bury him.'

As the deputy hustled Wood up the steps the sheriff turned to Malloy.

'Howdy stranger, name's Campbell, and this here's my deputy Will Euston. How do folk know you?'

'The name's Malloy.'

Campbell's eyes dropped to Malloy's Peacemaker, then he glanced at the palomino.

'Fancy piece of horseflesh,' he said. He jerked a thumb in the direction of the office. 'I got some questions, Mr Malloy.'

He turned away and went through the same door the deputy had taken Wood. Malloy looked along Main Street to where a large crowd had now gathered around the stagecoach. Then he stepped up to the boardwalk and followed Campbell.

'There's coffee on the stove,' Campbell said when they were inside the office. He went behind a scarred desk and sat down beneath an old railroad clock pinned to the whitewashed wall.

Malloy took down a tin cup from a hook and poured hot black liquid from a smoke-stained pot.

'You plannin' to take a look at the stage?' he said.

'Plenty of time for that. Tell me what happened.'

Malloy took the seat opposite the sheriff, his Plains spurs ringing against the wooden legs of the chair. He described the attempted hold-up from when he first saw the three men until the stagecoach had resumed its journey into town. When he'd finished Campbell eyed him carefully.

'You a lawman, Mr Malloy?' Again his eyes flickered over Malloy's Peacemaker.

Malloy shook his head. 'I was just ridin' into town, and saw what was happenin'.'

'Plenty of folks woulda kept low,' Campbell said.

Malloy shrugged. 'Guess if I'd thought long enough I'd have done the same.' He glanced around at the bills stuck to the wall.

'Any reward for these gunnies?'

Campbell shook his head. 'Not in this town. Maybe buy you a bottle of redeye. The name Marcus Kane mean anything to you, Mr Malloy?'

Malloy took a sip of the scalding coffee. Who the hell was Marcus Kane? He hadn't reckoned on the town band turning out but Campbell was sure acting strange.

'Sheriff, there's a wounded man down at the stage office,' Malloy said.

'I'll get to him,' Campbell said. 'The doc was with the stage. You ain't answered my question.'

'I don't recollect the name Marcus Kane.'

'Or Marcus Kane's brother Bart?'

Malloy put down the tin cup on the desk.

'Sheriff, you mind tellin' me what this is all about?'

'Those critters you brought in worked for Marcus Kane. They wouldn't have attacked the stage unless they'd been told to.'

Campbell looked up as the deputy appeared at the door that Malloy guessed led out to the cages at the back.

'Will, Mr Malloy wants to know about the Kanes.'

Euston crossed the office to pour himself coffee.

'The Kanes and a whole pack of side-winders are holed up a day's ride from here at Silver Creek. They've taken over an abandoned Army fort outside the settlement.'

'So what they aimin' to do?'

Campbell grunted. 'Most time they're puttin' the fear of God into the homesteaders. Threatenin' to kill 'em, then drivin' 'em off afore they're legally settled.'

'Why ain't they bein' stopped?' Malloy said.

Campbell snorted. 'Me an' Will are all the law this town's got. An' we've got just thirty-six square miles. We step out our patch an' we're just a coupla more townsfolk. We need US marshals but that ain't likely to happen durin' my time.'

'Save for his brother Bart, Kane's men come into town. They act proper an' we gotta leave 'em alone,' Euston added. He glanced at the sheriff as if looking for agreement. Malloy guessed Euston wasn't sure they could keep on holding the line.

'The Kanes aimin' to make money by bringin' in beef?' Malloy asked.

'They don't have to,' Campbell said. 'Good grass is getting scarce. We got a coupla spreads 'round these parts but they ain't big. The cattle barons up north want the old open range back. They're willin' to pay men like the Kanes to do their dirty work for 'em.'

Malloy nodded. First in Abilene, and later in Ellsworth, he'd seen cattlemen planning to bring their longhorns north from Texas. Their arrival was bound to put pressure on the rich bunch and buffalo grass to be found in these parts. The Union Pacific railroad bringing in homesteaders was increasing the rival claims for land. Malloy had even heard talk of sheepmen moving in.

'So why you tellin' me all this?' Malloy said. 'I'm plannin' to ride on through.'

'You're gonna hear about the Kanes from someone,' Campbell said. 'We wouldn't want a sharp feller like you on their payroll.'

'After I've cost him a coupla men?'

Campbell grunted. 'Caleb Wood an' that Colorado critter'll be no great loss to him. I heard tell Kane was gonna get rid of 'em anyways.'

Malloy got to his feet. 'I ain't denyin' I could do with earnin' some travellin' money but I ain't lookin' for trouble. I'm gonna rest up for a coupla days, and then I'll be ridin' north.'

Campbell stared across the desk at Malloy for a few seconds. Then he nodded.

'I'm gonna take your word, Mr Malloy. If there's money in your poke the Palace'll take good care of you. An' if you're a drinkin' man the Silver Lode ain't bad if you're partial to redeye. One final question afore you go. You see the critter that got away?'

'Big feller wearin' a reservation hat. No Indian, though.'

Campbell nodded. 'Figures. Injun Fletcher. Traded with the Shoshone until he went bad.'

'Thanks for the coffee, Sheriff.'

Malloy left the office and paused for a moment at the edge of the boardwalk to look down Main Street. In the time he'd been with the sheriff, the town had become busier. More women walked back and forth in front of the stores. A couple of drummers hurried along with their bags of samples. Hard-looking men in range clothes stepped along the boardwalks, their spurs jangling. A Shoshone, in moccasins and dirty dungarees, led a grulla down the street, the slate-blue of the horse's mane catching the sun's rays. A couple of young cowboys were tethering their mounts at the rail outside the Silver Lode saloon.

Malloy stepped down to the dirt and unhitched his palomino from the rail. As he rode at walking pace towards the livery stable he was aware of the curious glances from the townspeople. Maybe some looks weren't so friendly. Some of the folk were taking sneaky looks at the Peacemaker on his hip. He swore under his breath. Maybe they thought he was some crazy gunfighter from one of those dime novels he'd seen back in Houston. For a moment he hankered after the trail. Townsfolk could be difficult to get along with.

'Mr Malloy! Mr Malloy, sir! Over here!'

Malloy turned to look across to the boardwalk on his right. A tall man in a black suit stepped out of the shadows. At first Malloy thought he was a preacher but then the sunlight shone on the silver pin of the man's stock and on to the silk vest that gleamed beneath the long jacket.

Malloy halted his palomino. How did this well-heeled stranger know his name? He made no move to approach the man, resting easily on the horn of his saddle, his reins loose.

'The name is Walker, Mr Malloy,' the man called. 'I own the stagecoach. I'd consider it an honour if you joined me for a drink at the Silver Lode.'

A brief smile appeared on Malloy's face.

In the saloons of the trail towns he'd passed through he'd drunk only sour mash. Most of it, he reckoned, had been poisonous enough to draw a blister on a rawhide boot. Walker didn't look as if he'd be buying busthead whiskey, and maybe he'd know where Malloy might earn some travelling money.

'I'm gonna settle my horse and check in at the Palace,' he called. 'Then I'll be pleased to join you, Mr Walker.'

Half an hour later Malloy's big palomino was snugged down at the livery owned by a man called Haines who sported the largest moustaches Malloy had ever seen. Then, after he'd crossed Main Street on foot, he'd found the Palace fancier than expected. There was a hint that it had seen better days in the dusty long drapes at the tall window overlooking Main Street but the approach to the desk was well carpeted, and the desk-clerk neatly turned out. After arranging a room and mentally counting the dollars left in the pouch beneath his shirt, he'd been pleasantly surprised.

'A discount for helping our town, Mr Malloy,' the clerk had said.

Now Malloy pushed his way through the batwing doors of the Silver Lode. He looked around him. To his right stood tables

31

surrounded with rough wooden chairs. Among them, in a corner, sat a group of cowboys laughing loudly, too intent on having fun to pay him any attention.

To Malloy's left stood softer chairs and low tables and beyond them a faro table. The saloon must have been fancy at one time. Behind the table a staircase ran up to the floor above. Opposite from where he stood, across a space clear of tables, a bar ran the length of the rear wall. A fat cheerful-looking man, wearing a long white apron over dungarees, stood behind the bar polishing a glass. The barkeeper looked up and said something to the solitary figure resting his boot on the brass rail, his back to Malloy.

'Mr Malloy! My pleasure you could join me, sir!' Walker turned back to the barman. 'George, my bottle, please. Mr Malloy and I shall take a table.'

'Right away, Major.'

Walker led the way, stopping short of the faro table, and indicating that Malloy should take one of the leather chairs. George, who had followed, placed a bottle and two glasses on a low table between the two men, before returning to the bar.

For someone who owned a broken-down stage Walker was sure getting fancy treatment. Malloy watched as Walker unscrewed the bottle cap and poured two generous measures. He placed the bottle back on the table, slid his hand beneath his jacket and brought out two long cheroots. From the pocket of his woollen shirt Malloy took a wooden match, and flicked it across the sole of his boot. He lit Walker's cheroot. Then he lit his own, inhaling deeply. The sweet smoke rolled around his mouth. It sure beat Bull Durham. When he took up his new job he'd stick to smokes like these.

Blue smoke was drifting above the two men when Walker lifted his glass.

'Your health, Mr Malloy, and my thanks for saving the stage. I believe you'll find this whiskey to your liking.'

Malloy raised his glass. He paused, letting the fumes reach his nostrils. The harsh edge of sour mash was absent. A moment later the smooth spirit eased down his throat to warm his insides. He breathed deeply. The major – where did he pick up the rank, he wondered – was right. He hadn't tasted whiskey like this since that crazy night in Abilene when the devil himself seemed to be dealing him all the cards.

'Tastes good,' Malloy said.

Walker poured another two drinks, but

this time left his own glass on the table. Malloy did the same. Something told him he was going to need a clear head.

'What did you think of my stage, Mr Malloy?'

Malloy was silent for a moment. He was drinking Walker's whiskey, smoking his fine tobacco. This was no time to tell a man he should be spending money on a new stage instead of buying expensive liquor and fancy clothes.

'Guess it does the job,' he said.

Walker smiled briefly. 'I see you're a courteous man, Mr Malloy. I'm trying to establish a coach line between here and Cheyenne. The passengers today were personal friends. That old stage comes in handy for checking if the route is going to work out.'

'But I guess Marcus Kane ain't keen on that notion,' Malloy said. Seeing Walker's surprise, he added, 'Campbell filled me in.'

'Kane is aiming to take over this town, Mr Malloy. The cattle barons will bring back their beef, and ten years' work will be wasted. The silver was only ever low-grade and is almost finished, but we can still make out. Indeed, we can prosper again. But since the Kanes arrived we need more law than Campbell can provide. Campbell does his best but he's no longer a young man. A regular stage would get us attention from Cheyenne. Men would arrive willing to invest in the town again.'

Walker tapped the table to emphasize his argument. 'We've tried everything else, and so far we've failed. A regular stage line is the last chance for Masonville.'

'Folks just sitting around waiting for the Kanes to arrive?' Malloy said.

'They're not gunfighters. They're storekeepers, old miners, homesteaders driven off their land. They can't handle the Kanes.'

Malloy stared hard at Walker. 'An' you think I can?'

A slow smile appeared on Walker's face, and he leaned forward to pick up his glass.

'You've a sharp mind, sir. Four hundred dollars a month. More than the town pays Campbell.'

'You know nothin' about me, Major.'

'I spent twenty years of my life forming opinions about men, Mr Malloy. I'm willing to back my judgement.'

Malloy shook his head. 'Sorry, Major. If Kane is all you say he is then it'll take time. An' that's somethin' I ain't got. Sure I'd like to earn some money...'

Malloy stopped abruptly as something

35

moved at the edge of his vision. His head snapped around to see a young man in range clothes standing only a few feet away, his face flushed, and his eyes bright. Beyond him, the faces of the cowboys on the other side of the room were turned in his direction. Malloy guessed the young man had crossed the saloon from them.

Walker spoke first. 'Later, if you want a word, Jed, I'm busy now.'

The young man hitched at his belt. 'You ain't offering this stranger the job I should have, are you, Major?'

'The answer's still no, Jed...'

'How do we know this stranger ain't really workin' for Kane?' The young man swung around to face Malloy. 'Seems mighty handy to rid Kane of two men he was gonna kick out anyways.'

'Take it easy, feller,' said Malloy. 'I'm just here for a drink with the major.'

One of the cowboys called from across the saloon. 'C'mon, Jed! You're spoilin' the party.'

The young man ignored the shout, keeping his eyes fixed on Malloy.

'From what I hear, mister, you got lucky. Bushwhacked Kane's men when they made that run for the stage.'

36

For a few seconds Malloy stared across the space that separated him from the young man.

'I ain't a bushwhacker,' he said at last, his voice even. Then he shrugged, as if the young man's insult could be ignored. 'But, yeah, guess I got lucky.'

The young man shifted his feet in the sawdust of the saloon floor.

'Unless you was there waitin' for the hold-up. Had a tip-off from Kane. Make you a kinda hero round these parts. Supposin' I say you're playin' a four-flush hand? Kane coulda put you into this town as a spy.'

Suddenly the saloon was very still. The cowboys who had been talking among themselves fell silent, exchanging glances. Only the sounds of cheery greetings between two men in the street beyond the batwing doors penetrated the silence inside the saloon. Malloy sat unmoving, watching the young man whose left hand had dropped to his side, his right hand hovering above his sidearm.

Then Walker spoke. 'Don't be so damned stupid, Jed.'

He began to rise, but Malloy, without turning his gaze from the young man, laid a restraining hand on Walker's arm.

'I just happened along, young feller,' he said. 'A coupla days an' I'll be ridin' north.'

The young man's face flushed a deeper red, and his voice rose.

'Then why ain't the job mine?'

Malloy shrugged. 'None o' my business. Maybe the major here don't wanna see you dead.'

Jed took two rapid steps backwards. 'You sayin' I ain't good enough?' he shouted. 'I'm gonna show you how good I am! Get on your feet, mister!'

'Fer crissakes, Jed!' The yell came from one of the cowboys.

The flush of the young man's face had faded, save for burning patches above his cheekbones. Around his nose, pale skin was stretched taut above the thin line of his lips.

'You don't get on your feet, mister, I'm sayin' you're yeller!'

Weariness showed on Malloy's face. Inwardly, he cursed his decision to interfere in the attempted robbery of the stage. Pull a sidearm without a badge and some damn-fool gunny would be bound to happen along to try and make a reputation. He wished to hell he'd ridden north-east at the last fork in the trail. Masonville would have just been a town he might have heard about. Now it was too late. This young fool with too much liquor in him wasn't about to let go.

'Remember, you called it,' he said. He put down his cheroot on the low table, and stood up, his hand brushing the leather of his vest.

Through the dust motes picked out by the late morning sun a flash of silver arced across the space between Malloy and Jed. The small, flat throwing-knife buried itself into the top of the young man's arm. His gunhand froze inches from the butt of his sidearm. He let out a shocked cry of pain. Then his legs folded beneath him and he fell backwards to sit in the sawdust, as if someone had jerked a chair from beneath him. His head down, he began to swear through clenched teeth.

Malloy reached the bar in five paces.

'Gimme that cloth, George!'

The barman threw him a cloth, and Malloy dropped to one knee alongside the young man, feeling the spur on his right boot grazing the back of his woollen trail pants.

'Hold on, feller,' he said.

A quick pull, prompting a cry from Jed, and Malloy had the knife in his hand. He wiped it on the cloth, and then used the cloth to bind the wound.

'What the hell's goin' on?'

Malloy looked towards the batwing doors. Outlined in the light was the bulky figure of Sheriff Campbell, his Marshal Colt held loosely by his side. Behind him stood one of the young cowboys who, Malloy guessed, must have slipped away from the crowd in the saloon.

Malloy stood up. 'Nothin' to worry about, Sheriff,' he said. 'Young feller here got a little liquor crazy, that's all.'

'That's correct, Sheriff,' said Walker. 'Mr Malloy and I were having a quiet drink together.'

Campbell reholstered his Marshal Colt. He crossed the saloon to stand looking down at the young man who had remained on the floor, clutching the wound in his arm.

'I see you in here rest of the month, Jed Miller, an' I'll kick your butt from here to Cheyenne!' Campbell said. 'Now get over to the doc!'

Wordlessly, the young man scrambled to his feet, grabbed his hat from the sawdust and, his head down, quickly left the saloon.

Campbell turned to Malloy and Walker.

'That young pup's gonna get hisself killed one of these damned days,' he said. He jerked a thumb. 'Seems trouble's gonna follow you around, Malloy. Maybe the town'd be better off if you kept on ridin'. You wanna earn that travellin' money, go an' see Jack Peters. Tell him I sent you.'

'What's the job?'

'You'll find out. But it's one to get you killed if you ain't mighty sharp!'

CHAPTER THREE

Malloy broke from the stand of cottonwoods and urged his palomino into a lope. The couple of hours' sleep he'd snatched had set him up after the ride from Masonville. He sat easily in the saddle, a tall lean figure, his face shadowed by his Stetson.

In the late afternoon sun the leather vest over his trail shirt kept him pleasantly warm. His Peacemaker was at his hip, its holster secured with a leather tie-down. His flat throwing-knife, its handle bound with tight rawhide, nestled in his vest pocket. Close to his knee his Winchester long-gun rested in its scabbard.

Below him, about two hours' riding he guessed, the settlement of Silver Creek lay outlined against the bunch and buffalo grass. Beyond was the old frontier fort, its stone buildings commanding the surrounding country. Malloy guessed the Army had abandoned the fort after the 1868 Treaty with Big Cloud.

Kane had chosen well. The fort was easily

defended and would offer safe haven for his men. Yet if they had money in their pokes Silver Creek, with its saloon and calico queens, was close enough for a high-heel time.

A gust of wind brushed against his face, and the palomino lengthened its stride across the high meadow. Malloy pulled his Stetson lower and kept his eyes on the trail leading to the settlement.

Daylight was fading when Malloy left the hard ground of the trail, reining back as he reached Silver Creek's Main Street. Most of the stores flanking the street appeared to be abandoned. Rough planking had been nailed across many of the doors. A couple of old men moved along the boardwalk, their heads down, seemingly intent on minding their own business. From a large building some thirty yards down the street, yellow lights bobbed in the dusk as lamps were lit. Silver Creek's saloon, Malloy surmised, where some of Kane's men were sure to be found.

A few minutes later, having hitched his palomino to the rail, Malloy pushed through the batwing doors of the saloon. On his left the bar ran the full length of the wall. Over to his right stood rough tables and chairs. On both sides tall mirrors had been fixed to the walls to make the place look bigger.

Directly ahead of Malloy a swarthy man in trail clothes sat beside a pianola looking across at him. The pianola stood close to the foot of a flight of stairs. Malloy guessed they led up to where the women carried on their business. Malloy knew there'd be women. Around gunslingers with money, there'd always be women. But it was early hours and only men were in the saloon.

At one of the tables opposite the bar sat four card-players. One of the men wore fine clothes, a dark-blue vest gleaming in the lamplight beneath the smooth grey of his jacket. Highly polished boots beneath the table showed what could have been silver spurs. On a table close to the player lay a silver grey Dakota hat with its four-inch whipped brim. Unless some tinhorn had found his way to these parts Malloy reckoned he was looking at Marcus Kane.

Four men sat drinking beer beyond the players. Kane, if that's who it was, and the other players looked briefly in Malloy's direction then looked back down at their cards. A big man, his face half-covered with bushy whiskers, took his foot off the brass rail of the bar and half-turned to look his way.

Two Mexicans, Malloy guessed from their features, were behind the bar counter. The nearest one wore a long white bar-apron. The other stood opposite the bearded man. Malloy crossed to the bar, and put down a coin.

'Beer,' he said.

Without a word the bartender pulled down a tankard from the shelf behind him, and held it beneath the pump. Malloy watched the beer gushing from the tap. When white froth was bubbling over the sides of the glass, the Mexican lifted the tankard to the bar. Malloy made no move to pick it up.

'You got women here?' Malloy said.

'Off the trail, *hombre?*' The Mexican nodded in the direction of the other man behind the bar. 'See Mendoza.'

Malloy picked up his beer and moved further along the bar to the other Mexican.

'You got women in this place?'

Mendoza showed white teeth. 'Upstairs. All the women you want.'

Malloy raised the glass to his mouth and took the foam off the top of the beer.

'I'm minded to see the goods before partin' with my money.'

Mendoza nodded, showing his teeth again.

45

'Don't take too long. Or the Russian'll come and find you.'

The big bearded man alongside Malloy roared with laughter.

'Sure, cowboy! I come and get you!'

Malloy put down his beer, walked close to the cowboy near the pianola and went up the stairs. From the balcony above the bar he stepped through a doorway into a short corridor. Four doors, all closed, were evenly spaced along the right-hand wall.

Malloy opened the first. A woman was seated at a table, her back towards him, applying rouge to her hard face, which Malloy could see in the cracked mirror before her. She turned, her face showing no change of expression as Malloy closed the door and stepped back into the corridor. He opened the next two doors, only to close them promptly as other hard rouged faces stared back at him. Then he opened the last door and found what he'd been looking for.

On a bed in the corner of the room sat a young woman covered only in a rough shift. Her back was pressed hard against the wall, her knees were drawn up to her body, and the pale skin of her unrouged face showed red around her eyes. Malloy stepped inside the room and closed the door, staring hard at the young woman. Her eyes were screwed shut as if to blank out the world in which she found herself.

'Betsy-Mae Peters?' Malloy said.

The young woman's eyes opened, her mouth forming into an open circle.

'Yes,' she said eventually. Her voice was scarcely a whisper. 'Who are you?'

'You got any clothes 'sides that shift?' Malloy said.

He waited until Betsy-Mae shook her head.

'No matter, I got a coat and blankets. Stay here but you come when I call. I'm takin' you out of this place.'

Her eyes opened so wide with fear her eyeballs bulged.

'They'll kill you. An' the Roosian–'

'You come when I call,' Malloy cut in. 'You un'erstand?'

He waited until she nodded, then, as she began to scrabble across the bed, he turned on his heel and left her. He went back down the stairs, his eyes on the card-players but they seemed only aware of the cards falling from the dealer's hands. Malloy crossed to the bar and stood alongside the Russian.

'You like what you see?' Mendoza said.

The Mex sure liked showing his teeth.

'I got a hundred bucks for Betsy-Mae,' Malloy said.

For a moment Mendoza looked puzzled, then his smile reappeared, his teeth gleaming.

'Two days, cowboy. I throw in food, and any other woman you want.'

Malloy took a sip of his beer, holding his glass high.

'You ain't understood, Mendoza,' he said. 'I'm aimin' to buy Betsy-Mae outta here.'

'She ain't for sale!'

'Then I guess you're givin' her to me.'

Mendoza's eyes flickered towards the Russian. Malloy sideswiped the glass into the Russian's face, the shattered glass spraying blood and beer over the bar as the Russian fell like a tree on to the saloon boards. Malloy's left hand shot out, dragging Mendoza across the bar, before he spun around and brought up his Peacemaker.

Mendoza screamed as he guessed what was about to happen. Malloy's Peacemaker roared and the face of the cowboy who had dragged a shotgun from behind the pianola erupted in a gush of blood. Grey matter splattered against the wall behind him. Malloy shifted his aim and shot the unconscious Russian in his right shoulder.

'Fer crissakes!' someone yelled.

Nothing moved in the acrid air as the gunshot blasts bounced around the walls of the saloon until they were lost, leaving only the sounds of Mendoza's whimpering.

Then the card-player in the fine clothes put down his glass and stared without expression across at Malloy.

'An' what the hell you gonna do now, cowboy?'

The player alongside him spoke before Malloy could answer.

'I'll take him, Marcus.'

'Shut your godamned mouth, Bart,' Kane said, without taking his eyes off Malloy. 'No more killin', cowboy.'

Malloy tightened his grip on Mendoza.

'That's up to you, Kane.'

'So what is it you're after?'

'I'm takin' Betsy-Mae outta this place.'

Kane nodded. 'OK. What else you lookin' for?'

'Nothin'.'

Kane sat still for a few seconds. 'You tellin' me you shot two of my men to get a whore?' he said at last. 'Are you crazy?' The skin across Kane's cheekbones tautened. 'You musta rode in from Hicksville. You got four goddamned shots in that Colt. You ain't

49

gonna make the door!'

'Your glass,' Malloy said.

His finger curled around the trigger of his Peacemaker. The sounds of the weapon and shattered glass erupted as a white furrow splintered the surface of the card-table. Beyond the table a chair, struck by the heavy slug, skittered across the floor.

Malloy's eyes flicked up at the mirror to check the Mexican barman, then came back on Kane.

'Three left,' he said. 'The next between your eyes.'

Kane sat there staring back at Malloy, thin lips pressed together.

Malloy waited a moment, then he shoved Mendoza away from him, sending the Mexican staggering across the floor to fall against the pianola with a jangling crash. Without taking his eyes off Kane, he called out.

'Betsy-Mae! You come on down now!'

Above him there was the sound of a door closing. A few moments later Malloy heard the slither of a hand on the banister. From the corner of his eye he saw Betsy-Mae reach the bottom of the stairs.

Malloy swung his Peacemaker across the tables before aiming again at Kane. 'Any man says a word to Betsy-Mae, I'll kill him.'

He took a pace away from the bar. 'Betsy-Mae, you come an' stand behind me. Nobody'll hurt you. We're gonna walk out to the big palomino.'

Her shoeless feet silent on the boards, the girl crossed the saloon to stand behind Malloy. He jerked his sidearm at Kane.

'On your feet and over here,' he said. 'Make sure you don't cross in front of the table.'

Kane rose slowly from his chair, his eyes fixed on Malloy. He moved clear of the table, giving no chance for Bart Kane and the others to draw their sidearms unseen by Malloy. With deliberate steps Kane crossed the floor until he was a few feet from Malloy.

'Closer,' Malloy said.

Kane stepped forward. Malloy raised his Peacemaker and pressed the end of the barrel between Kane's eyes. His other hand pulled Kane's sidearm from its holster.

'You're walkin' out with us,' Malloy said. 'Your men try anythin', even they shoot me, you still die.'

Beads of sweat began to form on Kane's forehead.

'You hear that, Bart?'

'I hear it, Marcus.'

Feeling his way across the saloon, the soles of his boots pushing through the scattering of sawdust, Malloy edged himself and Kane towards the batwing doors. In his left hand he held Kane's sidearm loosely down by his leg. Behind Malloy, her hand clutching his belt, shuffled Betsy-Mae. Nobody in the saloon moved as the three pushed through the doors.

'Get up and sit close to the horn,' Malloy ordered the girl.

As if scenting freedom, Betsy-Mae swung herself nimbly on to the front of the palomino's saddle. Malloy sucked in the night air. If trouble was coming his way it would be in the next few seconds.

'Stand back two paces,' he ordered Kane.

As Kane shifted his weight backwards, Malloy swung up behind the girl and brought his Peacemaker to aim again at Kane. The expression on Kane's face showed that he knew he'd missed his chance.

'We're gonna walk real slow outta town to the west,' Malloy said. 'You better pray none of your gunnies wants you dead.'

Without a word Kane turned and began to walk down Main Street, Malloy checking his palomino at the same pace. The boardwalks on both sides of the street were deserted, and nothing stirred in the alleyways leading behind the abandoned stores.

Maintaining the walking pace, they left Main Street, heading west. Above them, the moon threw a pale light on to the trampled dirt of the trail but Malloy knew they were already lost to any observer back in Silver Creek. They'd gone maybe another 500 yards when Malloy broke the silence.

'This is far enough,' he said, halting his palomino.

Kane stopped and turned, the paleness of his face tilted upwards to Malloy.

'Man handles a gun that good could get rich.'

'Turn around, Kane,' Malloy said.

'A woman's gonna get you killed one day.' Kane shrugged and turned away from Malloy.

Malloy reversed his Peacemaker, leaned forward, and slammed down the butt on Kane's head. He swung down from his saddle, and grabbed the back of Kane's coat as Kane staggered and fell to his knees. Heaving on the coat, Malloy dragged Kane clear of the trail, and rolled him down the slope of a nearby gully.

'I've a pony stashed in a stand of cottonwood,' Malloy told Betsy-Mae when he'd remounted his palomino. 'We've got some hard riding ahead of us.'

CHAPTER FOUR

Malloy rested his hands on the horn of his saddle, reins loose in his hand, a faint smile on his face. Ten feet from his palomino Betsy-Mae was clasped in the arms of her mother. Both women were crying loudly, Betsy-Mae breaking off only to sob that she'd been so foolish and so bad. Close to the women stood Jack Peters, his face screwed up with pleasure, patting Betsy-Mae's back as if comforting a foal.

Betsy-Mae raised her head. 'You ain't gonna whip me, Pa?'

'No, child! That I ain't! Your ma and me ain't been right since you took off. Thanks be you're home. Now we're a family agin.' Peters looked up at Malloy. 'There's a hundred dollars in the Masonville bank, Mr Malloy. Got your name on 'em. I wish we had more. Annie and me, we owe you Betsy-Mae's life.'

Malloy raised one finger to his weather-stained Stetson, and began to turn the palomino's head. He'd earned his travelling money, now he'd be smart to get back to Masonville.

'Wait, Mr Malloy!'

Annie Peters had unclasped herself from her daughter's arms. Alongside the beanpole build of her husband she reminded Malloy of a small busy bird, still pretty despite the back-breaking work of the homestead.

'You ain't leavin' our home without good food inside you,' she said. She studied Malloy with intelligent eyes. 'An' you need a rest. You look plain tuckered out!'

Malloy looked down on the determined expression of the woman, her hands resting firmly on her hips. He touched his Stetson again with a finger. There were some women in the world you could never argue with. He reckoned Annie Peters was one of them. Anyways, she spoke good sense. He did need a rest from the saddle. Masonville was still several hours' riding. And how long had it been since he'd last sat around a family table and shared a meal? Too damned long, that was for sure.

He swung his leg over his saddle.

'Show me the well, Mr Peters. I'll get washed up.'

Even Betsy-Mae managed a watery smile to match the beaming smiles of her parents as they led the way along the track towards their rough timbered cabin.

Three hours later Malloy was back on the trail heading for Masonville. Annie Peters had sure made him welcome. When he'd seen the food spread out on the table, he'd protested that this was more than he deserved.

'We ain't puttin' small grub on the table, Mr Malloy,' Jack Peters had said. 'There ain't a man in Masonville who was ready to take on the Kanes like you done.'

But despite the good food and welcome break from the saddle his bones still ached. He was beginning to favour the job up north more and more. Getting that foolish young girl out of Silver Creek had gone well, but if he took on the Kanes once more he was likely to end up on Boot Hill. He snugged down in his saddle, content to let the palomino have its head, the horse covering the ground at a steady lope.

Ahead was the bend of the trail where he'd tangled with the three *bandidos*. For a moment his mind held the image of the fair-haired woman from the stage.

He'd like to have met up with her again. Her fingers had been bare. A smart lady like her would have worn rings if she was with a man. Had he been spending more time in Masonville, he'd have tried to make her acquaintance. Malloy shifted in the saddle as the palomino rounded the bend, its mane ruffled by the wind.

Goddamnit to hell! Cursing his own stupidity, Malloy's hand dropped from his reins. Too late, his curled fingers froze above the butt of his Peacemaker.

'Hold it right there, Malloy!'

A line of riders straddled the trail. Ten long-guns aimed for him, five each side of Bart Kane who stood in his stirrups astride a big roan. How the hell had they gotten ahead of him, even with his stopover at the Peters' place?

'You sure took your time gettin' here, Malloy!' Bart shouted. 'Now unbuckle that belt, an' maybe you get to live a mite longer.'

Harsh laughter erupted along the line of riders.

For an instant Malloy figured the odds. His long-gun was secure in its scabbard. But he knew he could roll from his horse and kill Bart Kane with his sidearm before he hit the dirt. That was a sure way of dying, he decided. The long-guns couldn't miss at this range. He dropped the reins from his left hand. Keeping his eyes on Kane, he felt for the big metal buckle at his middle.

'I ain't tellin' you again, Malloy,' Kane yelled. 'I ain't a patient man.'

Malloy eased off his belt. His Peacemaker, weighing over two pounds, dragged the leather down behind him across the cantle of his saddle.

Kane turned his head to give orders and two riders broke from the line to circle around the rear of Malloy. He saw that their trail pants were damp to the knees. Then the tang of their sweat and unwashed bodies reached his nostrils as the men closed him. His gunbelt was jerked away from behind him.

'Get your rope, Matt,' Kane ordered. 'We're gonna have ourselves a little party.'

The back of Malloy's neck turned ice-cold, and the muscles across his stomach tightened. A couple of years back he'd seen a rustler lynched by cowhands. The bulging eyes and the throttled gasps forced from the man's throat as he slowly strangled, kicking and swinging at the end of the dangling hemp, was something Malloy would never forget. Only death at the hands of the Comanche could be worse. He'd make them shoot him first. He still had his throwing knife. Get close enough to Kane and maybe he'd finish him.

Two nooses of rough hemp settled around his shoulders. He had an instant to suck in air before the rope tautened, hauling him from his saddle to hit the ground hard. His shoulder slammed into the earth of the trail, the side of his face smashing against the packed dirt.

Dazed, clawing at the tautened ropes that bit through the leather of his vest and the wool of his trail shirt, he struggled to his knees to see Kane dismounting.

'Hold the sonovabitch right there,' Kane roared. 'I got business with him.'

A voice called from the line. 'We ain't got time for this, Bart! You knows what Mr Marcus told us.'

Kane spun around to face the line. 'Shut your goddamned mouth!' His lips were flecked with spittle, his face blood-red. 'Marcus ain't gonna be back for a week or more.' He turned back to Malloy. 'Get that bastard on his feet, an' jest make sure he cain't kick out.'

Malloy, only half-conscious, barely aware of Kane's words, was hauled up from the dirt. One of Kane's men dallied the end of the rope above Malloy's spurs. Held upright only by the tautened ropes in the hands of the two men behind him, Malloy was unable to move his arms or legs. The salty tang of blood filled his mouth. Kane stopped two feet away, thrusting his mottled face towards him.

'Afore you part from this world, Malloy, I'm gonna make you a sorry sonovabitch for makin' a fool o' me in front of my brother.'

Malloy spat a full mouthful of blood into Kane's face. There was a snicker of noise from the line of men. Kane spun on his heel, scrubbing at Malloy's blood around his nose and mouth with the back of his leather glove.

'Shut your goddamned mouths!'

'Tol' you we dain't have time for this,' said a voice.

Kane sucked in air and swung with his clenched fist into Malloy's gut. Bile surged into Malloy's throat, combining with blood to choke him, as Kane struck him again. Malloy's legs tore against the rope. He tried again to spit but once more Kane's fist hammered into his gut. Blood and bile ran down Malloy's chin. The ropes tore at his body, searing his flesh.

The hemp held him trussed like a hog. Kane's face had turned ashen, his eyes rolling back in his head, as he swung his gloved fist again and again at Malloy. Through the swirling clouds of his mind, Malloy struggled with a final thought. I'm to be lynched by a crazy man. Then the rolling clouds darkened to black and he knew no more.

'There you go, Mr Malloy, suh. Few more days, no hard ridin', an' you'll be jest fine.'

Despite his huge fingers the big man deftly tied the last knots on the cloth bound around Malloy's middle. Dressed only in his trail pants, Malloy rolled over to sit on the edge of the bed, wincing as the pain shot across his chest and gut.

'Doc'll be along in a while to take a final looksee.'

'Don't recall him here at all,' said Malloy, which prompted a smile from the big man. 'I'm mighty grateful to you, Henry.'

'Aw shucks, Mr Malloy, I ain't done much.' Henry's teeth gleamed against his black skin. 'My old outfit, we all got taught some doctorin'. Kep' a lot of us alive. But I do say I coulda done with you not being such a big feller. Me carrying you to the privy these last days! Anyways, it's Cap'n Joe and his boys you should be thankin'.

Danged lucky the Volunteers happened along or you'da been dead meat by now.'

'Reckon you're on the mark there, Henry,' Malloy said slowly.

Not that he recalled anything of the Volunteers happening along the trail and saving his hide. Neither had he much recollection of the days that he'd been in the Walker house. A sudden thought struck him.

'Why'd Cap'n Joe bring me here?'

Henry shrugged. 'Cap'n found your old Cavalry papers in your boots, I guess. Anythin' Army around these parts gets brung to the major. When the major saw you in the back of that wagon he took you straight in.'

He grinned seeing Malloy's sudden grab at his boots where they stood beside his bed. 'Don't you trouble yo'self, Mr Malloy. Papers is on the chest.'

Malloy nodded, pressing against the hard notch within the boot, half-way down the length of smooth leather. He looked across the room. On top of the military chest sat the oilskin package he'd toted around these last five years. They'd probably saved his life. Without the special care he'd gotten these last few days he might not have come through.

'Doc's here, I reckon,' Henry said as the sound of voices penetrated the door. A moment later the door was opened.

'Howdy, Major,' Malloy said as Walker's bulk filled the doorway.

'Good day to you, Mr Malloy.'

For a second Malloy was conscious of Walker's glance resting on the black-and-green bruise marks showing above and below the tight bandage around his chest. Then Walker stepped aside.

Malloy jumped to his feet, ignoring the shaft of pain beneath the bandages. His hand swept up the grey blanket to cover his bare shoulders.

'Ma'am, you cain't come in here! We're...'

He broke off, red-faced, as Major Walker and Henry burst out laughing, leaving Malloy standing transfixed by the sky-blue eyes of the fair-haired woman from the stagecoach.

'Let me introduce you, Mr Malloy!' Walker said. 'Doctor Beth Blackwell's been looking out for you these past ten days.'

Malloy fell back on to his bed, the blanket still clutched around his shoulders, his face still burning.

'Can't recall meeting a lady doctor afore,' he said slowly. 'But I'm mighty glad to make your acquaintance again, ma'am,' he added hastily. 'Just a mite surprisin' meetin' like this.'

'The century's moving along, Mr Malloy,' Beth Blackwell said crisply. She turned to Walker. 'Abraham, if you and Henry would give me a few minutes I'll take a look at Mr Malloy.'

'You an' me alone?' Malloy asked quickly. 'Shouldn't Henry stay?'

A smile showed on her even features. Malloy noticed she had a dimple in her left cheek.

'I believe your honour is safe with the major just outside the door,' she said. 'We'll join him shortly.'

She waited until the two men had left the room, the door closing on their chuckles. Seems I'm well enough to be made a pilgrim of, thought Malloy. He wasn't sure if he felt pleased or not. Beth Blackwell approached the bed, a leather bag in her hand.

'You can take off the blanket now, Mr Malloy. Lie face up on the bed.'

'Oh, yeah. Sure.'

Malloy climbed back on to the cotton mattress, letting the blanket slip from his shoulders, aware that she was only a foot or so away from him. During the War women were often to be found in hospitals. He'd seen them helping the men, nursing them when ordered by the surgeons. But real doctoring? No, sir!

Then he remembered visiting the men in the field hospital after the hellfire of Dry Wood Creek. They too had been lined up on cots, as he now was, staring down at their blue pants. Some of them had pants legs flat on the mattress, and fear and horror etched in their eyes. He shook his head to drive the thoughts from his mind.

'Is anything wrong, Mr Malloy?'

'I'm jest hopin' you doctors have learned something these last fifteen years.'

'We keep trying, Mr Malloy.' Blackwell's fingers pressed gently on his skin.

His mouth twitched. Maybe having a lady as a doctor wasn't such a bad idea at all. Then he grunted aloud as she pressed hard against his chest.

'Take a deep breath,' she ordered.

He did so, and a stab of pain seared his chest.

'Cracked rib, I guess,' he said, feeling damned foolish.

Beth Blackwell's expression didn't alter.

'You're lucky. As far as I can tell you've no

lasting internal injuries. Henry tells me you're not passing blood.'

Malloy felt his face grow warm again. 'No, ma'am. Doctor.'

She rose from her chair. 'The rest and good food have probably done more than I have. Carry on applying the ointment for a few days, it'll help clear the bruises. The rib will eventually heal. Keep it strapped and don't do anything foolish to make it worse.'

She crossed to the pitcher on the table by the window. She poured water into the earthenware bowl and rinsed her hands.

'The major tells me you're taking a job up north.'

Malloy swung himself back on to the side of the bed, slipping his arms into the sleeves of his trail shirt.

'That's my plan,' he said. 'But maybe I can do something for the major afore I leave. Seems only fair.'

'You mean stay and help run the stage line?' Beth Blackwell said sharply. Her head was down and her back towards him.

He finished buttoning his shirt before replying. Now why had she come out with that notion?

'I wasn't thinkin' about that, ma'am,' he said. 'The major must have something else I can do for him. Anyways, first I have to pick up my money from the bank.'

She stiffened, and swung around to face him, water dripping from her clasped hands.

'Haven't you heard?' She shook her head as if to chide herself. 'Of course you haven't. The bank was robbed four days ago. Mr Stockin's cashier was shot dead. Aside from what people have hidden away there's not a dollar left in town!'

Goddamnit! The cards were stacking up against him. If the Kanes were hitting the bank they were getting mighty impatient. Maybe his first notion was the right one. He should keep on riding north. Masonville was proving more trouble than a horse with a notch in its tail.

'Were they Kane's gunnies who robbed the bank?'

'The major knows more than I do.'

As Malloy pushed himself off the bed and stood up to shrug on his trail vest his chest burned with the pain. He'd get used to it. He was just pleased it wasn't the rib he'd cracked a couple of years before. He'd got rid of that damned jughead roan as fast as he could. Once the rib knitted he could forget it. Even the ache in winter from the Johnny Reb minié had faded after a few years. He took four paces to the door and opened it. Half-way along a wide hall Walker and Henry broke off their conversation.

'I just heard about the bank, Major. Kane's men?'

'I'm sure of it,' said the major. 'Marcus Kane would order his brother to shoot anyone trying to break into his territory. Not that we'll ever pin the blame on either of the Kanes. The three hold-up men will have long gone from these parts.'

'Seems I lost my travellin' money.'

Walker shook his head. 'Sam Stockin's bank in Cheyenne will make it good. But it'll take time to transfer the money. Sam's been told Cheyenne wants to see Masonville a lot more settled than of late.'

'Even if that means Marcus Kane has finally taken over?'

A muscle twitched in the major's jaw. 'I guess that's about it.'

Malloy paused. Riding away from the beating he'd taken from Bart Kane would stick in his craw. But what the hell? Masonville was just another struggling town on the trail. Nobody could say he owed the town anything. Walker had taken him in but who knows what might have happened if he hadn't been around when those hold-up merchants attacked the stage? Picking up his money in Cheyenne would take no more than a few days. There was a good trail heading north from thereabouts. Maybe he should think about that.

Beth Blackwell had moved past him to stand alongside the major, and Malloy was suddenly aware of her steady gaze. She had the bluest eyes he'd ever seen on a woman. The morning sun shone gently on the fine fair hair that lay in curls on her forehead. His eyes dropped to her ringless fingers. She sure was a fine-looking woman.

'Major, you still reckon a regular stage will stop the Kanes?' Malloy said slowly. Although his question was to the major his gaze held that of Beth Blackwell.

'That's what I believe, Mr Malloy,' Walker said.

Malloy was damned if he couldn't see a flicker of hope show in Beth Blackwell's eyes. He realized then that she was as determined as the major to see the old stage reach Cheyenne. A slow smile showed on his bruised face.

'First time I been hungry in days, Major. I'm gonna need a steak if we're to talk about that stage line o' yourn.'

CHAPTER FIVE

Malloy leaned back from the table, sucking the sweet smoke into his lungs, the smoke from the cheroot rising above his head to curl around the oil-lamps suspended from the whitewashed ceiling.

'Your houseman knows his food, Major. I ain't eaten so well for a long time.'

'Juan returns the compliment, Mr Malloy. He says you speak Spanish like an *hidalgo*.'

Malloy dismissed the compliment with a wave of his hand. 'If I owned lands in the south-west I guess I wouldn't be ridin' north to earn a livin',' he said. 'We gonna take a look at your stage?'

Walker rose from the table. 'We'll walk across to the old barn. Beth Blackwell will join us when she's finished with Juan's little boy.'

Malloy stood up. 'Lady doctor takes some time gettin' used to,' he said. 'Though I recall some folks were arguin' about it during the War.'

Walker nodded. 'Beth's father was the

doctor here. He died a couple of years ago. William Blackwell was my closest friend. He was a distant cousin of Elizabeth Blackwell, the first woman in this great country of ours to qualify as a doctor.'

'I guess Doc Beth's tougher than she looks,' Malloy said.

'That's about it, Mr Malloy. William was determined his daughter would follow in his cousin's footsteps.' Walker looked around as Juan appeared at the door. 'An excellent meal, Juan. Please ask Henry to join us in the old barn.'

Juan bowed. '*Sí señor.*'

As Malloy and Walker crossed in front of the big house in the direction of the barn Beth Blackwell emerged from the small cabin on the other side of the paddock. The two men paused to allow her to join them.

'Enrico will be fine,' she told the major. 'The fever has broken. Would you mind, Mr Malloy?' She held out her bag for him to hold, and rolled down the sleeves of her dress. Malloy noticed the pale skin of her arms above the small but strong looking wrists.

They walked across to the barn where Henry met them at the high wide opening. The stagecoach was in a corner several feet in front of a wooden wall. They stepped through the straw on the floor of the barn and halted a few feet from the stagecoach. The light from outside fell on to its sides, highlighting the grey patches where paint had faded from the woodwork.

Malloy hesitated. At least in the saloon he and Walker hadn't had the evidence of the dilapidated stage before their eyes. The major had taken him into his own house and maybe saved his life. He'd have to choose his words carefully. Then he was surprised to hear Walker chuckle.

'No, Mr Malloy. I believe I know what you're thinking. Come the winter this stage will be kindling wood.' He turned to Henry. 'Time to show Mr Malloy our hand.'

Henry walked around the stagecoach. He grasped a large handle on what appeared to be the solid wooden wall and heaved. The wall swung back to reveal a further section of the barn. Henry continued to swing the false wall until he was able to secure it against the side of the barn. They stood silent for a few moments, gazing at what Henry had revealed.

Beth Blackwell broke the silence.

'Abraham, it's beautiful!'

'It sure is,' said Malloy slowly.

Before him the polished woodwork of a magnificent stagecoach shone in the rays of the sun penetrating the barn. The coach's red body shone above its yellow underside. The wheels, Malloy thought, were made of white oak. A finely painted landscape decorated the door nearest to Malloy. Leather curtains showed at the coach's sides, and through the open gaps Malloy could see small oil-lamps set above the plush of the seating.

'The finest coach of the Abbot-Downing Company!' Walker said proudly. 'One thousand and fifty dollars worth of the finest American craftsmanship.'

'This the Concord?' Malloy asked.

'You have it Mr Malloy! Strengthened with iron bands and resting on three-inch oxen-leather through-braces.'

'Does Marcus Kane know you have this?' Malloy asked.

Walker shook his head. 'I think not. I had it shipped in marked as furniture when Mrs Walker was alive. Outside this house only Sheriff Campbell knows it's here.'

Malloy was thoughtful.

'You get this even to the first station and the whole Territory's gonna be talkin' about Masonville. I'm beginnin' to see what you're gettin' at, Major.'

'Then you'll ride the one time, Mr Malloy?' Beth Blackwell placed her hand lightly on Malloy's arm.

Malloy grinned. 'Guess I don't stand a chance!' His grin faded. 'But I want you folks to understand me. One run only. I'm mighty grateful to you, Major, an' to you, Miss Blackwell, but I got a good job waitin' for me. I get my money from Cheyenne an' I'm gonna be ridin' north.'

'I expect to pay for your time, Mr Malloy,' Walker said.

Malloy held up his hand. 'No money. I get the chance to pay something back.'

'We'll take your offer, Mr Malloy,' Walker said.

'Then there's work to do,' Malloy said. 'Kane's not gonna rest. That business with the old stage and Betsy-Mae will 'ave made him jumpin' mad. We can try an' keep the Concord quiet 'til we're away from town, but word could get out.'

Walker nodded. 'We'll need a new messenger now Charlie Morgan's been wounded.'

'You know the folks 'round here,' said Malloy. 'Though I guess they ain't gonna be so keen since the hold-up. How far the first station?'

'Fifteen miles. All the stations are about fifteen miles apart.'

Malloy thought for a moment.

'The feller driving the stage the other day? He likely to be still willin'?'

'Cassidy will stay. He's the best whip around these parts,' Walker said.

'He ain't rattled by gunfire neither,' added Henry.

'OK, if the major can find a new shotgun that leaves the three of us to ride point.' He shrugged. 'We coulda done with four, but we'll manage best we can.'

'I think I know someone,' Beth Blackwell said. 'But I'll need to speak with him first.'

Malloy suddenly held up his hand.

'Someone outside!'

Henry rushed to the false door, ready to conceal the Concord as a figure appeared at the opening to the barn.

'Major! You there, sir?' The figure bent forward as if the speaker was peering the length of the barn. His voice sounded strained. 'We gotta whole heap of trouble!'

'Cassidy! You're meant to be with the team,' said Walker sharply.

'That's it, Major. I seen 'em. The whole danged team is sick! They ain't fit enough to haul a chuck wagon! An' they'll be like that for a time.'

'What's wrong with 'em?' Malloy asked.

'I ain't sure. I reckon they're poisoned. Some rattlesnake's put stuff in their feed. Tried some of it myself, sure tasted strange.'

Henry froze. 'The kid!'

'Henry?'

Henry turned to face the major.

'There was a young drifter up yesterday. Said he was lookin' for a job. I didn't like the looks of him at all. Sent him packin'.'

'This kid from Masonville?'

'Never seen him before, Mr Malloy.'

The major frowned. 'Henry, are you saying he poisoned the horses because we didn't give him work?'

'I guess that kid's in Silver Creek now, gettin' paid for his work,' Malloy said. 'You got other horses could do the job?'

'We've three in reserve,' Walker said. 'All the rest are out at the stations.'

'Three are all leaders,' Cassidy said. 'We're gonna need swings and wheelers.' The plug shifted in his mouth. 'We could try a spike team.'

Walker shook his head. 'No. We have to do this right.'

'Who else 'round these parts has horses good enough?' Malloy asked.

'Ebenezer Scroops,' Walker said. 'He runs fine horses.'

Cassidy cleared his throat, looked at Beth Blackwell, and didn't spit. The plug of tobacco shifted to bulge out his cheek.

'Scroops got the horses, Mr Malloy. Don't mean he'll sell 'em.'

'I ain't sure I'm followin' you,' Malloy said. 'Is he in with the Kanes?'

'Scroops is only in with Ebenezer Scroops,' said Walker. 'He does business only with hard cash. The bank hold-up will make no difference where he's concerned.'

'You tellin' me this Scroops won't take your note?'

'That's just what I'm saying, Mr Malloy.'

Malloy was silent. Sure, he'd offered to make one run with the Concord. But nobody had said anything then about sick horses. He looked at the grim faces of the three men, and the glum expression on Beth Blackwell's face. He hated to let her down but without horses there was nothing they could do. Then an idea came to his mind. Sure, it was crazy, but why the hell not try? Hadn't he always said on the Border that surprise was worth ten men?

'There's someone 'round these parts sure to have enough cash,' he said.

All three men exchanged puzzled glances before looking back at Malloy. Before any of the men could speak, Beth Blackwell stepped forward, placing her hand gently on Malloy's arm.

'Marcus Kane,' she said softly.

A shadow of a smile crossed Malloy's face.

'Ma'am, I guess you have to be real smart to be a doctor.'

Stars were sparkling like diamonds scattered on a sable blanket as Malloy rode his palomino through Silver Creek. When he'd come for Betsy-Mae nobody had known his face, save maybe for Injun Fletcher, and he'd been willing to risk Fletcher being in the saloon. This time he couldn't afford to be seen by any of Kane's men.

Through a gap between two storefronts distant lights flickered around the old fort. Close by, nothing stirred save for a dog scurrying across the street. Passing the saloon's doorway, Malloy kept his head down until he'd cleared the blast of hot smoky air. Jangling chords from the saloon's pianola and the screeching laughter of the hurdy-gurdy girls followed him as he again reached the shadows.

He turned his palomino, following the

directions to the livery given to him by Haines in Masonville. At that hour only the Creek's livery-owner should be about his business. Malloy wasn't looking for trouble. Risk his life every day and he wouldn't be around for long.

A flickering lamp at the side of a high open doorway threw light on to the livery sign-board. Malloy slid from his saddle, the reins in his hand, as a tall skeletal figure with a shock of black hair above his long face appeared from behind the door. In his raised hand a lamp flickered light.

'Just about to close up, mister. You lookin' to bed down your mount?'

'If you're Zeke Haines, I'm sent by your kinfolk over at Masonville,' he said.

'I'm Zeke. I'll give you a special deal.' Haines stepped forward. 'I reckon that...' He stopped suddenly, peering into Malloy's face now visible to him from the light of his lamp. 'Oh, my! I saw you ride out with Betsy!'

'Take it easy, Haines,' Malloy said.

He walked his palomino forward, the livery-owner backing along the wide straw-covered passage between two rows of stalls. Horses shifted, their hoofs stamping on straw, as the two men entered the barn. When

Malloy's palomino had cleared the doorway Haines put down his lamp on a wooden box.

'I'll close up,' he said. He passed alongside Malloy's palomino, and leaned his weight against the high wooden door. With a grunt of effort he shut out the night.

'You'll be OK here tonight, Mr Malloy.' Haines grinned, showing broken teeth. 'Yeah, I know your name, word gets 'round.'

'You ain't gonna get a passel of trouble?'

Haines's good nature shone from his reddened face.

'I'm gettin' outta here. Gonna join my brother.'

'You know when Marcus Kane comes outta the fort?'

'Kane's outta town. He's comin' from the east on the train an' goin' through to Cheyenne.'

Malloy swore softly. 'You sure of that?'

'I know it 'cos Strawberry Jack Wilson's to ride south to the railroad waterstop at sunup.' Haines pointed across the barn at a paint in one of the stalls. 'That's Wilson's horse. He's 'cross the saloon for the night with one of them women. Saves him goin' back to the fort.'

Malloy's muscles relaxed. For a moment he thought he'd risked coming into Silver

Creek for no good reason.

'You know why he meets Kane?'

'He totes a message pouch for him but I got no idea what's in it.'

Malloy frowned. 'Strawberry Wilson? How'd he get called that?'

Haines raised his hand to the side of his head.

'Wilson's got a red stain 'cross his face.' He peered intently at Malloy. 'You ain't gonna kill him?'

'Not unless I have to. I ain't in the killin' business. When's he come in?'

For a moment Haines hesitated.

'Just afore sun-up.' He pointed to an empty stall, larger than the rest. 'Put your mount in over there. There's a bunk at the back of the stall. It ain't the Palace in Masonville but it's OK.'

'I'm much obliged Mr Haines,' said Malloy. He fished out a handful of coins from his vest pocket. 'This enough?'

Haines's eyes opened wide. 'More than plenty, Mr Malloy. Privy's out back when you need it.'

Malloy spent some time bedding down his palomino in the stall before eventually lowering himself on to the straw mattress thrown down on the wooden bunk. He kicked off his boots, before placing his Peacemaker by his hat. Then he pulled the rough blanket over him.

'Sure gonna be a big day tomorrow,' he said aloud to the palomino. A minute later he was asleep.

'Mr Malloy!' Haines stood frozen in the early morning light at the entrance to the stall. His rounded eyes stared at the Peacemaker in Malloy's hand pointing directly at him.

'That was a damnfool move!' Malloy swung himself up from the bunk.

'I didn't mean...' Haines gulped. 'There's coffee on the stove. Coupla biscuits if you've a fancy for 'em.'

'Thanks, Haines. Coffee and biscuits sound fine.'

Malloy slid his sidearm into its holster, easing the leather on his hip and securing the tie-down. He stood up to pull on his boots, his fingers brushing the small notch in the leather. Then he settled his knife to where he liked it. The aroma of fresh coffee reached him from beyond the stall.

An hour later Malloy was against the wall of the barn inside the open doorway. As he watched Haines moving around the barn giving the horses their early feed he realized the liveryman reminded him of his own brother, good with horses, decent, and hardworking. He remembered Ned's puzzled expression when Malloy had told him he wouldn't be staying around.

Malloy breathed heavily through his nostrils. He wondered how his brother was faring. Had he now learned that their father's place wasn't big enough for two sons? As the elder, Malloy could have claimed the spread for himself. But newly back from the Army he'd soon realized it was Ned who was the one to get the Double M spread to what it was before the War. Ned would be the one to put on his best broadcloth for council meetings. He was the one to marry and have sons and maybe daughters of his own. His own future, he'd decided, lay elsewhere. His mouth tightened. Too damn late, by many years, for any regrets now.

Then he heard footsteps approaching and a low-voiced tuneless singing. He pushed himself off the wall and dropped his hand to his Peacemaker. Lamplight showed the angry red splash across the side of the man's face as he entered the barn.

'Haines!' the man yelled. 'You no-good Bible puncher! You got my horse?'

Malloy took two paces forward and slammed the barrel of his sidearm on to the man's neck. Wilson staggered and dropped to his knees on the straw. Malloy kicked out at his spine, sending Wilson sprawling.

Below Wilson, steel flashed, and Malloy jumped forward to slam down the heel of his boot on Wilson's wrist. He kicked away the knife with one boot, leaning forward on the other to press down hard.

'You wanna lose your chow-hand, make a move,' Malloy said.

Wilson shook his head, his face ashen against the red stain covering his nose and the side of his face. Fear showed in his bloodshot eyes.

'Close the door, Haines,' Malloy called.

As the liveryman appeared from the shadows and closed up the barn again, Wilson spat into the dust.

'Malloy'll not allus be here!'

Malloy took a rapid step to his left and lashed out with his boot at Wilson's knee, the pointed leather smashing at the bone. Wilson let out a choking gurgle of pain and clutched at his leg with both hands.

Malloy took a couple of paces back, his Peacemaker aiming at Wilson's belly.

'Get up.'

Cursing loudly, Wilson struggled to his feet.

'Drop your gunbelt,' Malloy ordered. 'You make a wrong move, an' I'll kill you.'

With shaking fingers Wilson fumbled with the buckle of his belt.

'I ain't aimin' to make trouble,' he said, as his sidearm fell to the straw.

Malloy lowered his arm.

'Where's the package for Marcus Kane?'

'Bart'll shoot me if you take that!'

'Then you've a real problem, Wilson. 'Cos I'll shoot you if you hold out on me. I ain't got time to waste. I'm gonna count to three. One.'

For a second Malloy saw indecision register in Wilson's eyes then his shoulders slumped.

'OK, Malloy,' Wilson said wearily. 'I'm gonna put my hand in my shirt.'

'Easy now,' Malloy said.

He raised his Peacemaker again as Wilson lifted his hand to undo a couple of buttons. He watched as Wilson fumbled beneath the rough cloth before pulling out a flat oilskin pouch.

'You mess with this, Malloy, an' we're both gonna be dead by sunset.'

Wilson pitched the pouch across to Malloy.

86

It landed in the straw a few inches from his boot. Keeping his eyes on Wilson, Malloy ran the toe of his boot across its surface.

'You know what's in this?'

Wilson continued to rub at his injured knee with a hand showing grimy knuckles.

'Papers,' he said with a shrug. 'Don't mean nothin' to me. I ain't been schooled.'

'Kane needs 'em for Cheyenne?'

'That's what Bart told me.'

'OK, how d'you get 'em to him?'

'I ain't sayin' no more...' Wilson stopped as Malloy raised his sidearm. 'Aw, to hell with 'em! I don't owe the Kanes nothin'. Ride south east of here for an hour. Cut through an arroyo and there's a trail going south. Coupla hours' hard ridin' an' you'll reach the railroad water station.'

'How long's the train wait?'

'Maybe thirty minutes. Critter rides shotgun for Kane takes the pouch. Hard sonovabitch from Kansas. Almost blew my head off once.'

'Kane got his own railcar?'

'Yeah, I'm told it's right fancy. But I never been inside.'

'How'd I know it?'

Wilson screwed up his hooked nose in thought.

'Got this fancy blue paint 'cross the top of the car,' he said at last.

Molloy nodded. Wilson had given him more than he'd expected. With his own rail-car Kane would be carrying money in a safe. He shifted his feet in the straw, continuing to gaze at Wilson with hard eyes.

Zeke Haines suddenly spoke from the shadows.

'Mr Malloy! You know what you gone an' tol' me.'

Wilson spat. 'What the hell's he sayin'?'

'He's a good man, an' he's hopin' I ain't gonna shoot you,' Malloy said slowly. 'Trouble is, I leave you alive and Bart Kane's gonna be after me afore noon.'

Wilson's head jerked up. Hope gleamed in his eyes. 'I ain't goin' back to the fort, that's for sure. Without the pouch Bart Kane likely turn me over to that Comanche half-breed.' He lifted his hands. 'Gimme a chance, Malloy! I'll ride west from here. Put a lotta country between me and Silver.'

'You don' have to kill him.' Haines called.

'Whatever you're gonna do is between you and the Kanes,' Wilson pleaded. 'I shoulda stayed away from 'em!'

Malloy raised his arm, staring hard at Wilson. Trembling, Wilson screwed his eyes

88

shut. Then Malloy lowered his Peacemaker to its holster.

'Haines! Get Wilson's horse. He's ridin' outta here!'

'Sure thing, Mr Malloy!'

Ten minutes later, Wilson swung up on his mount. Malloy moved alongside the paint to shove Wilson's gunbelt deep into his saddle-bag.

'You put a hand on that afore you're ten miles from here, an' I'll hear about it.'

Wilson shook his head silently and dug his heels into the sides of his mount. Then he ducked below the livery wall and rode into the early-morning light.

Malloy watched him go. Wilson would be no further trouble. He'd figured that if Malloy didn't kill him, Kane would. Wilson would keep riding until he felt safe. Malloy turned back into the barn.

He had to ride out of Silver Creek before the sun was any higher. He was pushing his luck already. But first he'd take a look at the oilskin pouch. He kicked his boot against the wood of the door. What the hell was in it that Kane needed so much?

CHAPTER SIX

Malloy had been resting for an hour, his back against the trunk of a cottonwood when the rhythmic beat of a railroad engine reached his ears. He shoved the short piece of jerky into his vest pocket and pushed himself to his feet. He gathered up the palomino's reins and hoisted himself into the saddle. His heels touched the animal's flanks and he moved slowly between the trees, his head and shoulders bent to avoid the overhanging branches. The steady rhythm of the engine grew louder. Malloy leaned forward to pull at one of his horse's ears.

'Seems we can't stay out of trouble just o' late,' he muttered.

For a moment he recalled the hard-eyed man from Dundee, Illinois, whose persuasive arguments had brought him northwards. Then the pulse of sound reaching him from beyond the ridge changed as the train began to slow. He pushed away his thoughts. In his mind's eye he could see the Union Pacific engine hauling the string of railcars moving towards the watering point.

Two hours before he'd ridden over the ridge beyond the cottonwoods to take a look at what he was going to have to do. The words of his old sergeant had come back to him when he'd reached the railroad.

If you gotta fight, son, make damn sure you know the ground.

The train would halt beside the water tank, its water fed from the wide stream that ran down the slope on the other side of the cutting. After a few minutes the conductor and the engineers would gather around the tank. Watering the engine took time. They'd be too busy to pay much notice to another messenger for Marcus Kane. If he could get past Kane's bodyguard he'd have the advantage of surprise.

Malloy eased his Peacemaker on his hip and leaned back to pull from his saddle-bag the pouch he'd taken from Jackson. Now it was packed with damp straw. He dug deeper into the saddle-bag to pull out a metal bar no more than two inches long. It fitted snugly into the left palm of his leather trail glove. When he closed his fingers over the pouch, its bulk covered the metal bar.

According to Jackson, Kane's private car was always to the rear of the train. He'd taken care to stride out the distance from the curve of the track to the likely position of Kane's railcar. If he'd calculated correctly, when he rode up to the bodyguard he'd be out of sight of the men around the tank.

But could he deal with the bodyguard out of sight of the passengers? If so, fine. If not, and they raised the alarm, he might just find himself shooting his way back over the ridge, and riding for his life. He'd heard that UP sometimes had guards all ready to go from freight cars.

From over the ridge the sound of metal screeching against metal and the hiss of discharged steam told Malloy the engineer had begun to apply the brakes. The high-pitched howl increased in pitch, then stopped abruptly. As if glad to take a rest, the engine emitted a long drawn out sigh of expelled air, then a further hiss of discharged water. Malloy heard shouts, and the engine noises dropped to a steady throb. The engine was alongside the tank.

He breathed in deeply, his fingers touching briefly the notch half-way down his right boot. He leaned forward to tug at the palomino's ear once more.

'Ain't a UP mount good enough to catch up with us if we can make it back here.'

He touched his heels against the horse's flanks and moved out of the cottonwoods and on to the top of the ridge, reining in to view the scene below, aware that he could be clearly seen by anyone who chanced to look in his direction.

The engine was standing alongside the tank over to Malloy's right. Around it clustered a number of men, all but one wearing greasy bib overalls. A tall man in a dark uniform, gold braid on his hat, was directing operations, shouting orders to three men who stood atop the engine holding the hose which led from the tank. Behind the engine a string of maybe twelve or thirteen cars extended beyond the curve of rail. Malloy walked his horse down the slope, sitting easily. Just another rider delivering a message to an important UP customer, his stance showed. Nothing for folks to get het up about.

He was half-way down the slope when the uniformed man, the conductor, Malloy guessed, stepped from the group and raised a hand in Malloy's direction. Malloy raised the pouch and pointed in the direction of the railcar with the fancy blue paint. The conductor barely paused before waving an acknowledgement and turning back to shout further orders to the engineers.

Ahead of Malloy the heads and shoulders of rail passengers showed through the car windows. Most gazed out without interest. One or two, probably from back East, pointed Malloy out to their children. Malloy saw that he'd be out of their sight, and that of the train crew, when he rounded the curve of the track.

His mouth tightened as he came alongside the two freight cars straddling the bend. Freight cars meant no passengers. But did they mean guards ready to pursue anyone crazy enough to hold up the train? He slowed his mount while straining to hear any noise from the freight cars but he could hear nothing. Satisfied, he turned his head, checking that he was out of sight of the engine crew behind him. Then he reined in abruptly, raising his hands level with the top of his palomino's head. The Frontier Colt aimed at him from the viewing platform of Kane's railcar was steady as a rock.

Hard against the railing stood a man in a city suit, wearing a brown derby hat. A coloured stone shone in his fancy necktie. Kane, it seemed, hired the best for his own protection.

'That's close enough, stranger!'

Malloy kept his hands in full view.

'Name's Denver,' he called. 'Gotta packet for Mr Marcus. You the feller from Kansas?'

'I'm Kansas,' he said. A frown knitted bushy eyebrows above cold eyes. 'Where's that dumb sonovabitch Wilson?'

'Gotta fever. So Bart tol' me.'

'He catch it from that Shoshone squaw he totes about?'

Malloy didn't change expression. Kansas might just have some brains under that fancy hat.

'You got the wrong feller,' he said. 'Strawberry's hitched with one of the calico queens from the Creek.'

A grunt of satisfaction came from the man, and he lowered the Frontier to slide it into its holster.

'OK if I drop my hands?' Malloy called.

'Yeah, and bring the pouch over here. I ain't getting down for it,' Kansas said. His hands touched the butt of his Colt. 'You tell Bart he's gonna get somebody killed, if he ain't more careful.'

Malloy began to move forward.

'Sure will. Hate to get myself killed over a dumb move.'

He reined in a few feet from the platform, estimating the other's reach.

'Gimme over the pouch,' Kansas said,

leaning a little further outwards to cover the distance to Malloy.

Malloy braced his legs against the irons of his stirrups and leaned forward, holding the pouch just short of the bodyguard's fingers. As Kansas reached out, Malloy let the pouch slip. Instinctively, the man grabbed for it, bringing his head forward.

Malloy threw himself across the palomino's neck and slammed his fist up beneath the man's nose. Gristle gave way against the metal bar in Malloy's hand. Reversing the direction of his swing Malloy slammed his weighted hand an inch below the brim of the derby hat.

As the bodyguard slumped over the rail Malloy swung out of his saddle on to the viewing platform, the palomino's reins held loosely in his hand. Once both feet were on the platform deck he stood still, his eye fixed on the door at the end of the short passageway, his hand resting on the butt of his sidearm.

Seconds ticked by. Nothing moved. He turned to hitch his horse with a quick turn of the reins around the metal rail. Then, bending to the jacket collar of the unconscious Kansas, Malloy hauled him out of sight of anyone passing the railcar.

He moved along the short passageway towards the closed door, not attempting to soften the sound of his footsteps. Anyone inside the car, he hoped, would assume that it was Kansas. He drew his Peacemaker, breathed in deeply, and pushed open the door, stepping quickly into the shadowy interior of the car.

On a purple *chaise-longue* ten feet from Malloy a struggle was in progress. The man's back was towards Malloy, his arms around the shoulders of a pretty young woman, locking her arms against his body. Over the man's shoulder, the woman's face was red with anger, her eyes tightly shut. Strands of blonde hair were dislodged from beneath her small hat. She opened her eyes suddenly, maybe hearing Malloy for the first time as he closed the door. Her eyes grew rounder. From her lightly rouged mouth came a tiny cry of shock.

'I told you to stay out until I called!'

The man disengaged himself from the woman, swung around sharply, and faced the door. He peered towards the shadows cloaking Malloy.

'What the hell's going on? Where's Kansas?' He released the woman who fell back against the cushions.

'Hold it there, Kane.'

Malloy stepped forward, his face still in the shadows, but with the sunlight filtering through the closed curtains glinting on the barrel of his sidearm. There was a gasp of fear from the woman. Kane dropped back on to the *chaise-longue*.

'You must be goddammed crazy!' Kane shouted. 'If UP don't hang you, I sure will! Come out of those goddammed shadows! I wanna see your face before it's at the end of a rope!'

Malloy stepped forward.

Kane's jaw dropped.

'I'll be goddammed! You crazy sonova-bitch! You here for another whore, Malloy? Take her!'

Stiff-armed, Kane pushed the woman away so hard she fell from the *chaise-longue* on to the floor of the car among a slithering of silks and a glimpse of high-button boots. She remained on her knees, ashen-faced, looking up at the two men, eyeballs protruding with fear.

'Get up ma'am,' Malloy said. 'Nobody's gonna hurt you. Sit over there and don't say a word.'

A mewing sound came from the woman as she scrambled to her feet and scurried across the car to a seat by the mahogany table.

'You use that cannon, Malloy, and UP men'll come through that door.'

'Sure they will. But then you ain't gonna be around to see it.'

Kane shrugged, his face showing no emotion.

'You tired of living then, Malloy?'

'Your men cleaned out the bank in Mason-ville. Hundred dollars of mine were sitting there. I want 'em back. Save me a ride to Cheyenne.'

Kane pulled up his face in mock amazement, turning to call across the car.

'Hear that, whore? This dumb sonova-bitch'll have me and the UP gunnies fightin' over his hide for the sake of a hundred dollars.'

Kane looked back at Malloy.

'First time I thought you were just crazy. Now I know different. You're not only crazy, you're cheap.' Kane pointed across the railcar. 'There's a hundred dollars in the poke on the table. Take it an' get off this goddammed train.'

Malloy stepped forward a couple of paces.

'I ain't finished. Bart had Major Walker's horses poisoned. The major needs eight hundred dollars to replace 'em. I'm puttin' that down to you. An' I'm here to collect.'

'That Concord Walker thinks he's gonna run, ain't gonna take him anywhere. He's dreamin', an' so are you if you reckon on gettin' that sorta money. Take the century.' He spat on to the woollen carpet. 'Try an' live long enough to spend it.'

The sound of the engine whistle penetrated the railcar. Malloy took two paces forward. Before Kane could move Malloy lashed out with his left hand. There was a crack of metal on bone, and Kane fell back against the cushions clutching his hand. A low moan of pain forced itself between clenched teeth.

Malloy stood over him.

'Next time I'll break it. I'm gonna ask you agin, Kane.'

Blood ran down Kane's chin from his bitten lip.

'I'll see you in hell first.'

Malloy raised his left hand.

'I ain't got much time Kane.'

'The safe's back of the book cupboard,' the woman blurted out. 'There's a stack of currency bills. I saw them yesterday.'

'You spyin' bitch!' Kane yelled.

Malloy took two steps back from Kane.

'The key! Where's the key?'

Again the woman spoke.

'In the pocket of that fancy vest he's wearing.'

The barrel of Malloy's Peacemaker pressed below Kane's ear, cutting off his curse, forcing him back against the cushions. Malloy's hand went beneath Kane's unbuttoned coat and pulled out a short-toothed key from the lower vest pocket. He tossed it to the girl.

'Open it up!'

Without a backward glance at Kane she rushed across the cabin and sank to her knees. Malloy heard her pulling books from shelves and he stepped back so he could see both Kane and the woman. Leather-bound books were piled to one side before the open safe.

'Oh Glory be! There's thousands of dollars here!'

Over her shoulder Malloy could see the stacked currency bound with brown paper straps. From the other end of the train there was a loud hiss of steam and the short sharp sound of the engine whistle.

'A thousand dollars. Not a dollar more! An' be quick!'

'The straps are marked! Here!' She

scrambled from the floor and thrust five packages at Malloy. He pushed four beneath his woollen shirt before turning back to Kane, who remained unmoving on the *chaise-longue*, one hand supporting the other.

'You called the lady a whore, Kane. I'm payin' her off for you.'

He tore the strap off the package in his hand, counted off a hundred dollars and handed it to the woman.

'You reckon you can hold on to that?'

She nodded. 'I've kinfolk on the train. I'll be safe with them.' She bit her lip. 'I ain't what he says I am, mister. I thought he was a gentleman. But all this money–'

'You've earned it! An' don't be so damned foolish again!'

Malloy swung back to face Kane.

'You show yourself outside this car, Kane, afore the train moves, an' I'm gonna have a long-gun on you.' He paused as if a sudden thought had occurred to him.

'Cassidy lost his timepiece when your gunnies held up the stage.' His hand jerked the Albert chain and the turnip watch from Kane's vest. 'I reckon you oughta settle with him as well.'

Two strides took Malloy through the door. He paused to look around, before checking that the bodyguard remained unconscious. He swung himself over the rail and into his saddle, pulling out the knot in his reins with a single pull. Then the palomino's mane was flying in the wind as Malloy surged up the slope. He crested the ridge as behind him freight car doors sounded. He swung around, but no horsemen burst from the train.

He'd have been surprised to see them. Kane, himself, would be aiming to settle with Malloy. If talk got around that Kane was being made a fool of, it wouldn't take too long for his gunnies to fade away, and that included his brother. As Malloy reached the cottonwoods he heard the train begin to move. A few minutes later he settled the palomino into a lope as they reached the level ground.

He'd be back in Masonville maybe by tomorrow nightfall. Walker could buy fresh horses, and the hundred dollars he'd earned were back in his poke. But something nagged him. How did Kane know about the Concord? Maybe that young pup Miller had been right. Kane could have a spy around the major, and he had to be close.

CHAPTER SEVEN

Malloy came out of the room wearing only his trail pants, scrubbing his dark hair with a rough towel. He walked along the corridor to where Henry was standing on a small stool, winding up a mahogany-cased wall clock.

'Major sure knows how to live,' Malloy said. 'Cain't be many houses these parts with a tub inside the house.'

'No suh. Mrs Walker, God rest her kind soul, insisted 'pon it. "Major Walker," she'd say, "bein' out West don't mean we have to drop standards."'

Malloy smiled. 'When's the major back from the station?'

'Some time afore nightfall I reckon. He's gone to warn 'em about maybe changin' our plans.'

'Then he's got good news waitin' for him!'

Malloy entered his room opposite from where Henry was stepping down from the small stool.

'You wanna hand with that fresh bandage?' Henry asked.

'Thanks Henry, but your nursemaidin' duties are over. Reckon I can manage.'

'Then I'll go find Cassidy an' we'll ride over to Scroops 'bout the new horses.'

'Sure thing, Henry.'

Malloy picked up the fresh bandage, made from torn clean cloth, off a heap left for him by Beth Blackwell. A female doctor! He still had problems with that notion. He remembered the expression on her face when she thought he was about to kill the *bandido*. Then how she looked when she sat beside his bed feeling for his cracked rib.

He blew out air through pursed lips. How did she see him, he wondered. As a drifter who earned his travelling money with a gun? Sure, he was useful to have around. If he got the Concord to the first station he'd achieve what she and Walker wanted. Then what? Aw, hell! He hauled the bandage taut around his chest with an abrupt tug, grunting with pain. Beth Blackwell stood for the modern world, and it was moving forward at a hell of a gallop. He'd better make damned sure this century didn't leave him behind.

He buckled on his gunbelt, and pulled on his boots, letting his fingers touch the notch in the leather.

'Mr Malloy!'

Malloy stepped out of his room. Henry was hurrying back along the corridor, a worried look on his face.

'That no-good Jed Miller's down by the little corral. Says he's got business with you!'

'He liquored up?'

Henry shook his head.

'Looks sober to me.'

Malloy grimaced. 'OK, Henry, I'll go see him. You get over to Scroops's place.'

What the hell did Miller want? Was he still trying to make a reputation? Was he intent on removing Malloy so he could claim the job with Walker? Crazy young pup. What was it the sheriff had said? Maybe Malloy should do Campbell's job for him and kick Miller all the way to Cheyenne.

He reached the entrance door of the big house and picked up his Peacemaker from the hook inside the door. The big short-gun slid easily into its holster as he stepped outside and went down the steps. Astride a fence-rail, 500 yards away, sat Jed Miller, his grey tethered alongside him. He slid to the ground watching Malloy approach, his hands held away from his body.

Malloy halted at a distance that he

favoured. No point in taking chances, although the kid didn't appear fired up or anything.

'OK if I take something outta my vest, Mr Malloy.'

'Slow an' easy, kid.'

'It's only paper, Mr Malloy.' Jed took from the pocket in his vest a single sheet of paper. 'Doc Beth gave it me.'

'What's it say?'

Jed coloured. 'Cain't tell you exact. My letterin' ain't so fancy. But I know what's in it,' he added hastily. 'Doc Beth thinks I'm good for ridin' point on the major's stage.'

'That right arm o' yourn's gonna be stiff for days.'

'It's good enough for ridin'.' Jed stood up straight. 'I'm as good with a gun in my left. I'll damned show you, Mr Malloy!'

'Come over here and gimme the letter.'

'Sure thing.' Jed stepped forward.

Malloy, his hand resting lightly on the butt of his Peacemaker, watched the young man approach. A faint flicker crossed his face as he saw Jed was taking care to hold his hands well away from his body. The kid was learning. A mighty surprising woman, Beth Blackwell. Keen that a *bandido* shouldn't be shot down, but willing to send Jed Miller to a job that might just get him killed.

Malloy took the sheet of paper handed to him. His eyes glanced down at Beth Blackwell's comments. Jed Miller had got it about right. Malloy shoved the paper into his vest. If Beth, as he was beginning to think of her, was willing to give Jed a chance, then he'd go along with it.

'OK, Jed. I find you ain't up to the mark, I tell you, an' you walk away from here. No talkin', no arguin', just nothin', you understand?'

'Sure thing, Mr Malloy. You got my word.' Jed beamed with pleasure. 'Where do we start... Fer crissakes!' His eyes bulged at the Peacemaker in Malloy's hand.

'We jest started,' said Malloy drily, easing his sidearm back into its holster. 'You walk up to a feller you ain't sure of, you keep an eye on his gunhand. C'mon, we'll take a walk beyond those trees.'

He turned to call out in Spanish to Walker's house-man who was carrying a pitcher of milk in the direction of the house.

'Juan, tell anyone around we'll be shooting for a while.'

'*Sí, señor.*'

'Jed, you bring that long-gun o' yourn,' Malloy ordered.

108

He led Jed to the small stand of cottonwoods, some hundred yards from the corral,
pausing briefly to break off a stout straight
branch from one of the trees. The two men
threaded their way through the trees until
they reached a small meadow. Malloy halted
and looked around. A natural bank was
maybe fifteen feet away.

'You got anythin' for a target?' Malloy
said.

Jed put one hand to his neckerchief.

'Wipes OK?'

'Sure.'

Jed carefully grounded his long-gun, and
untied the neckerchief from around his
throat. Malloy took it from him and tied the
cloth to one end of the branch.

He slipped his knife from beneath his vest
and sharpened the other end of the branch.
Judging the distance from where Jed stood
watching, Malloy paced out the ground. He
thrust the pointed stick in the ground. Then
he walked back to stand behind Jed.

'You got any notion that gettin' shot at by
the Kanes ain't what you want in this world,
then now's the time to say it,' Malloy said.

Jed's face was set. 'What you want me to
do?'

'I'm gonna drop this knife. When it hits

dirt, and not before, aim and fire.' He held up his hand, as Jed reached for his Navy Colt now switched to his left side. 'Sidearm stays on your hip.' He moved forward again, so Jed could see both him and the target.

Jed braced his feet on the grass, his face set.

'All ready, Mr Malloy!'

Malloy dropped the knife. Maybe the knife didn't touch dirt before Jed pulled the trigger. Maybe it did. Malloy wasn't sure. Beyond the drifting smoke, fragments of Jed's neckerchief floated on the light wind over the lush grass of the meadow. Staring hard in the direction of the target, Malloy showed no change of expression. He turned back to Jed.

'OK, pick up your big fifty.'

A large grin splitting his face, Jed holstered his sidearm and bent to pick up his fifty-calibre Sharps rifle.

Malloy pointed skywards with the knife to where a hawk had been circling for the last few minutes looking for small prey in the lush meadow.

'Hit that now!'

Jed tossed the long-gun from its vertical position, took aim and fired. The hawk exploded in a shower of feathers. Jed tossed the rifle back to the vertical and spun around to face Malloy.

'Godamn! I'm good, ain't I?'

Malloy looked at him for a long moment, struggling to keep a grin from his face. Crazy young pup! Feller could shoot though, no arguing with that. But no matter what Beth thought, only he could decide. Had Miller enough stomach to go up against hardened men like the Kanes and the short-trigger trash who rode for them?

'I'm gonna show you something,' Malloy said. He handed Jed the knife and walked over to where Jed had previously stood lined up with the target. Malloy stood loose-limbed, his hands at his sides. 'When you're ready,' he said.

A slow smile appeared on Jed's face.

'OK,' he said, and dropped the knife.

Malloy threw himself to the left, rolled on the ground on one shoulder, and blasted the remaining rags of cloth, his Peacemaker held rigid ready for a second shot.

'Jumpin' rattlesnakes!' Jed exploded.

Malloy was back on his feet, his sidearm reholstered.

'OK, now you try.'

Jed stepped forward, his thumbs in his belt.

'Sure,' he said. Then he stopped, and shook his head. 'I cain't do that. An' I ain't gonna shoot my foot off tryin'.' His face set as if he'd decided to show no emotion at the expected refusal by Malloy to take him on. 'I guess that's it,' he said soberly.

'I ain't said that,' said Malloy.

Jed's face brightened. 'Let me show you somethin', Mr Malloy.'

Now what was the kid thinking?

'OK,' Malloy said. At least he'd have a few more moments to think whether he was going to gamble with this young man's life.

He watched as Jed paced the distant to the target, and hung his hat over what remained of the stake. Then the young man returned to stand close to Malloy. Again he grounded his long-gun. Then to Malloy's surprise, Jed unbuckled his gunbelt and lowered it to the grass. He turned to face in the direction of his hat atop the stake, his hands tugging at the points of his leather vest.

'You wanna drop that knife again, Mr Malloy?'

Malloy dropped the knife. Steel traced through the air from Jed's vest to bury itself into the hat, pinning it to the branch. Malloy gazed at the quivering knife handle.

'I been practisin',' Jed said. 'Since the

saloon. What you reckon?'

Malloy closed the few yards to Jed. His fist flashed up, deliberately striking a glancing blow to the side of the young man's chin, but strong enough to dump him on the grass. Malloy looked down at Jed's startled face.

'That's for cussin' me in the saloon! Wait around for Henry. Tell him you're joinin' us. An' tell him I've gone into town.'

'Yes, sir! Right away, sir, Mr Malloy!' Jed scrambled to his feet, happiness lighting his face.

'An' one thing more. You keep your mouth shut you're with us. I ain't aimin' for Kane to know what we're about.'

'Yes, sir, Mr Malloy!'

Jed rushed across to the stake, grabbed his knife and hat, skittered back to scoop up his belt and long-gun, and charged away from Malloy in the direction of the house, whooping and hollering.

'Damn crazy kid,' shouted Malloy, and then laughed aloud.

An hour later he was in town, inspecting the racks of guns in Bridge's gunshop, being closely watched by Arnold Bridge. Malloy had heard that Bridge had worked as a gunsmith in Europe before trying his luck out West.

'Stocks o' guns ain't so high as they useta be,' explained Bridge. 'Folks around here bein' short o' money, an' all.'

There was a faint interrogative note in his voice that Malloy detected. He held no hard feelings. Bridge, he knew, had a wife and four sons. Malloy guessed that along with many of the storekeepers he was worried about Stockin's bank losses.

'I ain't sold my saddle yet, Mr Bridge. There's a hundred dollars in my poke an' another hundred down in Cheyenne. Soon as the bank reckons it's safe to move, they'll be here in Masonville. An' if I ain't around to collect it...' Malloy paused for a second. He'd only make a fool of himself to mention Beth's name. 'Then Sam Stockin will have it for you,' he finished.

'I hope you didn't think I was doubtin' you, Mr Malloy.'

'No, Mr Bridge,' Malloy said. 'But I ain't sure you got the hardware I'm lookin' for.'

Instead of replying immediately, Bridge came from behind the wooden counter to cross the store floor and pull down the blind. Only the light of the midday sun shining through the narrow entrance door now illuminated the store. Bridge took from his waist a bunch of keys, and returned to his post behind the counter. He selected a single key and turning to his rear, slipped the lock on a wide double cupboard. Then he threw back the doors with a flourish.

'This the kind of hardware that'll take your fancy?'

Malloy stood still, staring at the row of glistening Winchester long-guns leaning on mahogany supports, their stocks interspersed with Colt handguns, a strong chain running through the trigger guards of all the weapons. Maybe thirty in all, Malloy guessed, even numbers for Winchesters and sidearms.

'Plumb takes my breath away, Mr Bridge.'

'I got ammo to back 'em up. A smarter feller than me had a notion 'bout the rifling. Both long-gun and sidearm take the same slug.'

'I'll take...' Malloy broke off, as an animal scream penetrated the store. The midday calm of Main Street was shattered with the sound of hoofs thumping on the loose soil. There was a rattle of buggy wheels and the sound of a galloping horse.

'What the hell...?' Malloy was at the door in two paces.

A small boy in dusty britches pointed down Main Street.

'Doc Beth's horse done bolted!'

'I'll be back, Mr Bridge,' shouted Malloy over his shoulder, as he tore his reins from the hitching-post and flung himself into the saddle of his palomino, digging in his heels. Head held high, its hoofs briefly skittering in the soil, the horse took off down Main Street, its dilated nostrils feeling the wind that ruffled his mane. Ahead of him, breaking from Main Street to the rougher ground of the trail out of town, he saw Beth's buggy veer from side to side as she attempted to rein in the spooked pony.

'Let her run!' Malloy yelled, hoping his voice would be heard over the noise of the clattering wheels. Damn fool woman! Might know something about doctoring but she sure knew nothing about horseflesh.

The gap between his palomino and the buggy closed steadily.

'Just hold the reins tight and let her run,' he shouted again.

He saw her glance behind, aware for the first time that he was approaching fast, now that the pony's wind was beginning to fail. Her face was pale, but determined. With a forward thrust of his reins he urged his horse to greater effort. Fifty yards on he drew level with the pony's head. Dropping his right hand from his reins, he leaned over and caught the pony's headstall in his gloved hand.

With his left hand increasing pressure on the palomino's head he brought both animals out of a gallop, slowing them to a steady canter. Shouting a final order, Malloy halted the pony alongside his palomino.

For a moment the two animals and the two people were quiet as if all four were regaining their breath after the chase. Malloy ignored the stab of pain in his chest as he turned around in his saddle.

'You OK, ma'am?'

Colour was returning to Beth Blackwell's cheeks, the reins now loose in her hand. She nodded without looking up as if composing herself. Her blonde hair was loose, tangling in the breeze. Malloy noticed for the first time a dusting of fine hair on her cheeks, a golden tress by her ear. She must have sensed his gaze because she looked up suddenly, her blue eyes meeting his.

'Pony'll be fine now,' Malloy said.

He turned the head of his palomino and moved to the rear of the buggy. Leaning forward, he hauled out the small mornal from behind the seat where it was stowed alongside the leather medical bag. He slipped from his saddle and walked to the pony's head. Pulling down on the headstall he strapped on the feedbag.

'We'll give her a little time. She'll feel better after she pads out her belly awhile,' he said. 'I took on young Jed,' he called over his shoulder. His lips tightened. 'I hope he stays alive!'

'I'm glad. Jed might have gone the same way as Bart Kane, Mr Malloy. I didn't want that to happen.'

'How d'you mean, ma'am?'

'Bart Kane used to live in Masonville. He worked at the mine until the company cut down on the men, then he just drifted. He was always in trouble with Sheriff Campbell. Two years ago he was in a gunfight with cowboys visiting from up north. One of them shot Bart in the chest, and he almost died. The first time Marcus Kane saw Masonville or the Creek was when he came up from Cheyenne to see Bart.'

Malloy did some quick figuring. 'Was it you or your father who saved Bart's life?'

'I don't judge my patients, Mr Malloy.'

Malloy shook his head. 'I wasn't reckonin' that.' He bent and pulled up a handful of grass from the side of the trail. 'I was thinkin' of lotsa men who took a slug. Surgeon'd take

118

it out. Everythin' seemed fine, then the man wouldn't make it.'

She nodded. 'We've still a lot to learn, Mr Malloy.' She leaned forward to pat the flank of her pony as Malloy scrubbed off the sweat from the pony's sides with a handful of grass he'd torn from the side of the trail.

'Bart bein' his brother an' all, Marcus must feel he's in your debt,' Malloy said.

A pink flush appeared on Beth Blackwell's cheeks.

'Perhaps,' she said shortly.

'Maybe it's more than that,' Malloy said. Hell, now why did he have to say that?

Her lips tightened.

'I have to get back, Mr Malloy. I've Lucy Jones in my home. She's very sick.'

For a moment Malloy stopped unbuckling the feed-bag from the pony's head. Had he heard right? Lucy Jones in Beth's home? Maybe he'd made a mistake.

'That the calico queen – beg pardon, ma'am – the Texas gal from the saloon?'

Beth Blackwell opened her mouth but before she could speak Malloy held up his hand.

'You don't judge your patients, I guess.'

She smiled, waiting until he'd tossed the feedbag into the buggy, and then raising her

119

eyebrows as he took a quick turn of his palomino's rein around the rear of the buggy.

'I'll drive back into town. Make sure the pony's settled,' he said.

He stepped up to take his seat beside her, and she edged along the bench to give him space. As he turned the buggy to head back into town he was aware of the softness of her skirt brushing the wool of his trail pants.

He held the pony in a steady walk. No point in rushing, he decided. He tried to remember the last time he'd ridden with a lady in a buggy like this. There was that one time in Denver, he decided. But he reckoned that didn't count because the lady in question was the mayor's wife. And that sure was a crazy thing to do, anyway. The mayor had threatened to gun him down, and damn to the law. This was better. Maybe he could find a reason to take a buggy ride with Beth Blackwell again, some time.

'The major's houseman tells me you speak excellent Spanish, Mr Malloy.'

He shrugged. 'I did a year down in Texas with the Rangers. Most fellers down there gotta few words.'

'That's not what Juan said...' She broke off suddenly as they both watched the single horseman approaching them at a gallop.

120

'Now what's the sheriff all fired up about?' Malloy said.

Campbell reined in his horse, his words spilling over each other.

'There's a heap o' trouble at the big house. You two'd best get there. An' be quick!'

Malloy exchanged a quick look with Beth Blackwell. Then he cracked the reins across the pony's flanks.

CHAPTER EIGHT

Sam Stockin met them in front of the big house. On each step leading to the entrance door there were splodges of wet blood.

'Major got bushwhacked! How he got back here, I'll never know.' The banker's eyes above his thick moustaches were blurred with grief. 'He needs you bad, Beth.'

Without a word she stepped down from the buggy seat to grab her bag and hurry into the house. Juan the houseman approached, his dark features distorted with shock.

'Take care of the buggy, Juan,' Malloy ordered in Spanish, jumping to the ground. He turned to Stockin. 'It don't take much figgerin' who's behind this, but did the major see the bushwhacker?'

Stockin shook his head.

'Abe can barely speak. Got himself on his horse and rode three miles back here.' He put his hand on Malloy's arm. 'Abraham Walker's kept this town going, Mr Malloy. Marcus Kane will take us over now, for sure!'

Malloy looked over Stockin's shoulder as Henry appeared at the entrance door.

'Mr Malloy,' he called. 'The major's just said your name.'

Malloy went up the steps two at a time and followed Henry across the wide entrance hall and down a narrow passageway to a closed door.

'Doc Beth's still with him,' Henry said. His brown eyes softened. 'I tol' him about the new horses. But...' His voice trailed away. He turned from Malloy and tapped gently on the door before opening it.

Malloy stepped past him into the room. The room was large. Thick drapes at the window fell to polished boards that surrounded a richly decorated carpet. A huge canopied bed occupied the centre of the room, alongside which Beth Blackwell sat on a long-legged chair high enough to keep her level with the bed. There was blood on the stuff of her dress.

Walker lay, half-propped against thick pillows, his eyes closed. A white sheet spotted with blood was pulled stomach high. He was bare to the waist, with white swathes of cloth, heavy with blood, against his chest. As Malloy approached the bed Beth Blackwell looked up and shook her head slightly.

Malloy could see that Walker had been hit with rounds in the upper chest. The bubbles in the blood on his mouth told Malloy his lungs had gone.

'Malloy here, Major,' he said clearly.

Walker's eyes were moving around as if searching for someone or something. His mouth moved and Malloy bent his head to put his ear against the major's mouth.

'Will you ... will you ... the sor...'

Malloy turned to look at Beth Blackwell. He didn't understand, and his eyes asked questions of her. Again she shook her head.

Malloy turned back to Walker. His face was very pale and the moisture in his eyes was fading. Walker started coughing, a deep wet cough, and Malloy knew his chest was filling with blood, and soon he would drown. Malloy couldn't think of what to do or what he could say.

Walker's face was going slack and his eyes had closed, and then Malloy remembered something a surgeon had told him during the War. The last sense to go, the surgeon believed, was hearing. Malloy leaned closer to Walker's ear.

He spoke in a loud clear voice.

'Major! This is Malloy. Me an' Henry are gonna drive your Concord to Cheyenne.

124

One day real soon there'll be a Walker Stage Line.'

Did something show on Walker's face? Then Malloy felt the soft hand of Beth on his arm. He turned to see a solitary tear running down her cheek.

'He's gone,' she said. 'Ask Henry to come in.'

Malloy nodded wordlessly. He crossed the room to open the door.

'Henry, Doc Beth needs you.'

He stood aside to let the big man enter, and closed the door behind him. What the hell had he just done? He'd made a promise to a dying man he wasn't sure he could keep. But there was no shame in that, if he did his utmost to keep that promise. He wouldn't be counting the cost or thinking of his own plans. He owed that much to the major.

In his rush to enter the house he'd failed to leave his Peacemaker at the door. Instinctively now, his hand dropped to the butt. He strode along the passageway, and crossed the wide hall. Beth and Henry would be out later. Now there was no place for him here. He crossed the wide hall and halted at the entrance, looking down at the upturned face of Sam Stockin. Malloy shook his head, and heard Stockin curse.

'Tell 'em I've gone into town,' said Malloy.

He slipped his reins from the back of the buggy, threw himself into the saddle, and rode away from the house without a backward glance.

'Any o' Kane's men around?' Malloy asked.

The deputy, Euston, stood on the boardwalk, looking down as Malloy hitched his palomino to the rail.

'Three I ain't seen before playin' cards in the Lode. I jest taken a beer. What you so fired up 'bout, Malloy?'

'You ain't heard the news?'

'I just got back into town. Been checkin' on a homesteader.'

Malloy didn't wait. He snatched the thirty feet of hemp off his saddle, bounded up the steps to the boardwalk and headed for the saloon, his boots echoing loudly on the rough planks. Fifty paces took him to the batwing doors which he set swinging with a slam of his hand. As the wood swung back against his shoulder he stood, with the sun behind him, the hemp held in his left hand.

The saloon was almost empty. George was behind the bar polishing glasses. A solitary hurdy-gurdy girl was sitting alone at a table drinking from an earthenware beaker. She raised her eyes, hope showing briefly, as Malloy's eyes met hers. Then fear showed on her face as she sensed trouble. She stood up quickly, pushing back her chair, and turned to scurry past the faro table and out of Malloy's sight.

Over at the back of the saloon, opposite the long bar, three men were seated around a table, cards in their hands. Bottles and glasses stood amongst cards and poker chips scattered across the table. One of the men looked up from his cards and stared across at Malloy as if aware for the first time that he was watching them.

All three men, Malloy saw, wore rough trail shirts, leather vests, and sweat-stained hats. Two wore woollen pants, similar to Malloy's. The other, sporting long moustaches, wore moleskin pants, and his boots, Cavalry fashion, were visible beneath the table to a few inches below his knee.

Malloy covered the distance to the table in four fast strides. All three men looked up as he halted in front of them.

'You trail-trash know who I am?' Malloy said.

The three men laid their cards on the table and exchanged glances with each other.

'I ain't seen you in my life, before,' said the one with moustaches. 'But I tell you somethin', stranger. You insult me agin, an' you gonna pay for it.'

'The name's Malloy.'

With one swing of the coiled hemp he sent bottles and glasses flying from the table. Cards and poker chips flew into the air before falling into the rough sawdust. The three jumped back, kicking over their chairs, cursing as they reached for their sidearms. Flinging aside the hemp, Malloy thrust two hands beneath the table, lifted it shoulder high and charged forward.

As if hit by a battering ram, the three men went down into the sawdust, their sidearms torn from their hands. Malloy shoved the table aside. As the moustachioed man reached for a knife, Malloy took a quick pace forward and kicked at the man's knee an inch above the top of his boot. There was a sharp crack as Malloy's pointed boot drove into bone. An anguished scream echoed around the saloon, and the man lay still clutching his leg.

'You gonna pay for this, Malloy!'

Malloy leaned forward and cracked the speaker across the chin with the barrel of his Peacemaker. He watched the man fall, eyes rolling back in his head as he slumped into the sawdust. Then he swung around to press his sidearm against the forehead of the man on his left who had scrambled to his knees.

'You got five seconds,' Malloy said. 'Who bushwhacked the major?'

The man's eyes bulged with fear.

'I dunno Malloy, I swear it! Fer crissakes don' shoot me!'

'Two seconds,' Malloy said.

'Fer crissakes, Malloy!' He held up his hand, pointing at the man clutching his leg. 'He knows! Dutchy knows!'

Malloy reckoned he was scared enough to be telling the truth. He pulled his sidearm away from the man's head, and rapped it against Dutchy's leg. A gurgle of pain forced itself through gritted teeth. He forced his Peacemaker against the man's moustaches.

'You got the same five seconds.'

'I know hell!' Dutchy snarled defiance at Malloy. 'I heard Bart talkin' 'bout it, that's all!' His eyes were bloodshot with pain. 'Go ahead an' shoot, you ain't gettin' anymore!'

Malloy took a couple of paces back, eased his sidearm into its holster, and picked up his rope.

'I ain't gonna shoot you, Dutchy. I'm gonna lynch you!'

'You ain't gonna do no such thing, Malloy!' From behind him the shout came from the doorway of the saloon. 'Now keep your hands where I can see 'em!'

Slowly Malloy turned on his heel to look towards the batwing doors. On one side of the entrance stood Sheriff Campbell, his Marshal Colt hung loosely in hand down by his leg. On the other stood Will Euston, a long-gun aimed directly at Malloy.

'There's gonna be no vigilante law in this town as long as I'm sheriff. You reach for that cannon an' Will'll shoot you down.' Campbell raised his Colt to motion Malloy away from the three men struggling to their feet.

'Will! Run these sidewinders outta here. They can have their guns out o' town.' Again Campbell gestured with his Colt, this time at Dutchy limping towards him. 'You tell Marcus Kane all his men are now posted. You're too much danged trouble.'

As the deputy lowered his long-gun to cross the saloon and scoop up the sidearms from the sawdust Campbell raised his Colt.

'Hold it there, Malloy, 'til these no-goods are outta here.'

Breathing heavily, Malloy did as he was ordered, watching silently as the men were ushered into Main Street by Euston. Campbell stood there until apparently satisfied that his deputy was well clear of the saloon.

'Over at the jail, Malloy,' he ordered.

Campbell's gun was loose again down by his leg. Malloy reckoned he could shoot him twice before he raised the Colt. Sure he could, and then he'd be no better than the murdering son of a bitch who'd bushwhacked Abraham Walker.

'OK, Sheriff. Nice an' easy.'

Campbell stood back from the door, slipping his Colt back into its holster. Malloy passed him close, and stepped into the sunlight of Main Street. A knot of people had gathered on the boardwalk on the other side of Main Street opposite the saloon.

'OK, folks,' Campbell called. 'Nothing to get het up about. Me and Mr Malloy just goin' across the office.'

They walked the hundred yards to Campbell's office, the sheriff maybe a pace behind Malloy and a little to his right.

'The door ain't locked,' Campbell said.

Malloy shoved open the door and stepped into the shadowy office, warm from the pot-bellied stove in the corner.

'Get yourself some coffee,' Campbell said, picking up his pipe from the desk.

'No thanks.'

'Malloy, get yourself some goddamned coffee,' said Campbell. 'Then sit in that chair.' He pointed at the one in front of the desk. Without waiting for Malloy's reaction the sheriff walked behind the desk and sat down.

Malloy blew air through pursed lips. 'Maybe coffee's not a bad notion,' he said.

He crossed to the stove and poured coffee into a tin cup, then crossed to sit in front of the desk as the sheriff placed two shot glasses on his desk, before rummaging around in a drawer. Campbell grunted as he found what he was searching for. He kicked the drawer shut and put a bottle on the desk.

'You know what that is, Malloy?'

What the hell did Campbell think he was up to? There was a bushwhacker roaming around, and the sheriff was sitting around like the last time asking damned fool questions.

'Looks like firewater on somethin', he said.

'The finest Scotch whisky in the world, Mr Malloy. My old pappy, God rest his soul, brung fifty bottles out West from the ol' country.' Campbell puffed on his pipe. 'Cavalry'll charge the guns after drinkin' this. An' yet if a man's so all-fired up he cain't see sense it brings peace to his soul.' Campbell leaned forward and poured Malloy a generous measure. 'Tell me what you reckon on it.'

Malloy picked up the glass of amber liquid. The smell sure was different from any whiskey he'd come across, even the fancy stuff he'd drunk back East. He threw back the shot glass, the liquor smoothing down his throat to light a warming glow in his belly. Maybe the sheriff's pappy knew what he was about.

'Take another, Mr Malloy,' Campbell said, putting his own empty glass down. 'But this time take it slow. An' we'll drink to a fine man's memory.'

Malloy watched Campbell fill the two glasses. They raised them and sipped after Campbell had said clearly.

'Abe Walker, God rest his soul.'

Malloy put down his glass.

'I wasn't hell bent on any necktie parties, Sheriff. Just tryin' to throw a scare into those no-goods. Get 'em talkin'.'

Campbell puffed a cloud of smoke above his head. If he paid much attention to what Malloy had just said he gave no sign of it.

'You thinkin' of stayin' around?'

'Maybe for a while.'

'Then I gotta proposition for you, Mr Malloy. I knowed you been an Army man. You ain't got a gunslinger's brand, so I got you marked as a lawman sometime. How d'you fancy a deputy's job? I'm retirin' next year an' though Will's OK he ain't in your class. This job'd be yourn for the takin'.'

'Even with the Kanes runnin' Masonville?'

Campbell's lips tightened.

'Goddamnit! We're gonna miss the major!'

Malloy leaned forward, his arms on the desk.

'Listen, Sheriff. I'm willin' to back the major's judgement. Get a regular stage runnin' and there'll be enough support from Cheyenne to stop Marcus Kane. You've seen the Concord. We run that to the first station an' back again word'd soon get around. Build up people's confidence. They hear about it in Cheyenne, no tellin' what might happen.'

'Me an' Euston...'

'You both got enough here in town,' Malloy said. 'But I do need a feller ridin' shotgun with Cassidy. Cap'n Joe's Volunteers are all family men. They're needed here.'

Campbell puffed smoke for a while. Then

he stood up suddenly.

'Wait here, Malloy. I gotta notion.' Without waiting for Malloy's reply Campbell hurried out of the office.

Three minutes later he was back with Captain Joe Farmer, the grizzled old soldier who led the Volunteers. Maybe after all, Malloy thought, he had the name of one of the young men of the Volunteers.

'Howdy, Captain Joe.'

'Howdy, Mr Malloy. You're sure lookin' better than the first time I saw you.'

'You gotta name for me, Cap'n?'

The old soldier chuckled.

'How'd Joe Farmer suit? Reckon I can still handle a scattergun if needs be. Gettin' kinda dusty 'round these parts with the Kanes stirrin' up trouble, an' all.'

Malloy looked at the sheriff. How the hell was he going to get himself out of this barrel of tar without hurting the old soldier's feelings?

Maybe Farmer guessed what he was thinking, for his face set firm.

'Mr Malloy, I'd seen thirty-five summers when Johnny Reb came over the hill at Pine Bluff. This shotgun job gonna be tougher?'

'I sure as hell hope not, Cap'n Joe!' Malloy grinned. 'You got yourself a job.' He looked at Campbell. 'Euston around? He should know what I'm about.'

The sheriff shook his head.

'No point to it. I'll tell him, but he'll be gone in a coupla hours with Caleb Wood for the Cheyenne cage.'

Malloy nodded. 'OK, this is what I'm aimin' to do.'

The two men listened carefully as Malloy outlined his plan.

CHAPTER NINE

The fiery rim of the sun was showing on the horizon when Malloy, carrying his new Winchester from Arnold Bridge, entered the Haines livery stable. The big double doors had already been opened, and as he stepped inside the barn the pungent tang of horseflesh reached his nostrils. Along the row of stalls to his right, horses shifted in the straw beneath their hoofs as they became aware of his presence.

Haines, with the moustaches, came from the rear of the barn to meet him, leading Malloy's palomino.

'Mornin' Mr Malloy. I put new plates on your mount, like you tol' me. No rush for the money, we're all hereabout workin' on a book since the bank got hit.' He was suddenly sombre. 'Bad business about the major, God rest his soul. Guess you'll be shiftin' to the big house out there for a while.'

'Reckon that's about it, Mr Haines.'

'You gotta big ride today?'

Malloy shrugged. 'Thought I'd look

around. Maybe ride over to the Peters's place. I ain't really sure.'

Malloy slid his Winchester into its scabbard. No point in telling folks what he really intended. He glanced at the large round-faced clock above the entrance to the barn. Cassidy would be back of the big house about now with the Concord. Henry would be checking over the new Winchesters Malloy had bought from Bridge. Captain Joe and Jed Miller would join the stage at the edge of town.

Malloy placed his hand high on the palomino's rear leg before sliding it down to lift up the hoof.

'Mighty fine job on these plates, Mr Haines. I'm obliged.'

He let the hoof drop, took the reins from Haines, and heaved himself into the saddle. Horses whinnied as he walked the palomino the length of the barn and out into the light of the dawning day. The palomino skittered a few paces as Malloy turned the horse's head in the direction of Main Street and the trail out of town.

'Take it easy,' he said aloud. 'It's gonna be a long day.'

Save for the blacksmith stoking the embers of his overnight fire there was little movement around Main Street as Malloy walked the palomino past the storefronts. He rode past the last clapboard beyond which he could see Beth's darkened home. Missy, her maid, would be up and about at the back of the house. He turned his eyes away back to the trail leading away from town. His mind had to be on getting the Concord to the first station. As the palomino left the soft soil of Main Street, Malloy kicked the horse into a lope.

Two hours' steady riding took him to a point on the trail below a stand of birch trees breasting a ridge. He was satisfied this was the place he'd marked on the major's map for Henry and Jed Miller the previous night. He urged his palomino up the steep slope, digging his heels into the animal's flanks as it fought its way up the incline, snorting air from its widened nostrils.

Reaching the edge of the ridge, beyond the birches, Malloy commanded a view that took in both the country towards Silver Creek, and with a slight turn of his head, a view of the trail leading from Masonville. Riders approaching from either direction would be clearly in sight for several miles. Malloy slid from his saddle and looped his reins around the horse's foreleg, limiting the animal's ability to wander but still having enough freedom to move around.

He untied the strap of his canteen, and pulled his Winchester from its scabbard. The bark of the birch was rough against his back as he lowered himself to the ground and placed the long-gun on the grass beside him. He took a twist of jerked meat from his pocket, and swigged some water. He reckoned on having an hour or so before the Concord would appear. Any threat, and he'd be able to give plenty of warning.

An hour or so passed. Nothing moved beyond the arroyo and another stand of trees, maybe a thousand yards from where he sat. He slid his knife from his vest pocket to whittle a stick, and was just beginning to wonder if something had gone wrong at the big house when he saw the dark shape appear from the direction of Masonville. The recent rains kept down the dust.

He tossed away the stick, pocketed his knife, and pushed himself to his feet. His horse had retreated between the birch trees, and Malloy brushed aside thin branches to sheath his Winchester and secure his canteen. He swung himself into his saddle.

Ducking low over the horse's neck he walked the palomino between the birches to the rim of the ridge. The Concord was clearly visible now, Cassidy and Captain Joe seated alongside each other behind the six horses. Henry and Jed were riding maybe five yards each side of the swaying stage. As Malloy watched, the stage closed enough for him to hear shouts, urging on the leaders.

Malloy grinned. Cassidy had promised the rig would be at the first station before nightfall, and Malloy guessed the whip had decided on a fast start, ready to slow the team further along the trail when Malloy would be riding to join them.

He turned to scan the ground towards Silver Creek. Nothing moved. He was betting on the Kanes assuming any attempt to run the Concord would be delayed until Walker was given a decent burial. Both Sam Stockin and Beth had been a mite uncomfortable with his plan. But Henry and Jed, once he'd explained, knew he was right. This way, telling only those who had to know, would give them a chance of making the run undetected. News would travel fast if they made a successful run.

But he knew he wouldn't feel easy until they were some distance along the trail. Marcus Kane had known about the Concord. Not only that. Walker had told him

141

that the trial run with the old stage had been known to only a few people. So how had the *bandidos* known when to arrive?

He stood up in his stirrups as if to push the question from his mind until later. Even at this distance he could see the big smile on Jed's face. The kid had got what he wanted. Malloy's mouth tightened. He just hoped Jed had the guts to go with his ability to shoot.

The Concord drew nearer. Scroops might be ornery but he was honest. The wheelers next to the coach, weighing in at 1,250 pounds each, sure were fine horses, maybe even finer than the swings and leaders ahead of them.

Malloy raised his hand to acknowledge the raised arms of Jed and Henry, before turning again to scan the horizon. Nothing moved. He turned again to wave the Concord on, lowering himself back down in his saddle. His plan was to wait a further hour. Anyone attempting to come upon the stage from the rear would then be caught between two lines of fire. He looked around once more but the ground to the horizon was clear.

The minutes ticked by. Between regularly checking the view towards Silver Creek Malloy watched the Concord until it was lost to his naked eye. Yet again he scanned the ground towards the east. There was no sign of riders appearing from Silver Creek. Time to join the stage, he decided. He pulled the palomino's ear.

'You got some movin' to do, old feller.' He leaned well back in his saddle, his feet thrust forward as he prepared to ride down the slope to the trail.

Then he saw a dark shape move over by the stand of trees.

'What the hell?'

He swung around in his saddle, one hand on his rein, the other dropping to his long-gun. His eyes scanned the ground in the direction of Silver Creek. A short distance from the stand of trees, maybe 1,000 yards away, the figure of a man staggered around, his hands clasped to the side of his head.

What was a man doing afoot in these parts? Instinctively, Malloy thought of a trap, some scheme dreamed up by the Kanes. But a single man afoot? That made no damned sense at all. The man called out, his voice just reaching Malloy on the breeze. There was no point in taking chances. He reached into his saddle-bag and pulled out his brass spyglass. He raised it to his eye, gave the eyepiece a couple of quick turns and brought the man into focus, moving the spyglass as the man staggered around. Godamnit! Euston, Campbell's deputy! Was that blood marking the side of his face? While Malloy watched, Euston fell to his knees, his hand now held high in a signalled appeal for help. Malloy didn't move. His task was to see the Concord safely reach the stage station.

Yet he didn't aim to leave any man who needed help, especially a man who'd worked alongside Campbell. One day he might find himself afoot in open country, just praying some stranger would come riding by. Then Malloy remembered Campbell telling him Euston was leaving Masonville with Caleb Wood, who'd attacked the old stage.

Damned fool deputy had been tricked by the looks of it, Wood long since gone. Malloy thrust his spyglass into the saddle-bag and turned the palomino's head. Leaning back in his saddle, his legs thrusting forward, he urged his palomino down the slope.

Malloy eased back on his rein as the horse reached the foot of the slope, turning the animal in the direction of Euston. The deputy was back on his feet but still staggering around before the stand of trees.

'Hold it there, Euston!' Malloy shouted.

'You're gonna be OK!'

He closed the gap rapidly, halting his horse a few yards from Euston who still clutched his head.

'Thank hell it's you, Malloy,' Euston said through gritted teeth before taking two uncertain steps.

Malloy slid from his saddle. 'Take it easy. Lemme see that wound.'

He stepped close to Euston who lowered his hands from his head. Malloy turned the deputy's head with his hands. A deep gash ran down the deputy's face but Malloy could see it was clean. There'd be a scar but Beth could fix it.

Euston slumped forward, and Malloy grabbed him by both shoulders, throwing his own weight forward to prevent them both falling to the ground. Euston, seemingly revived, jumped back, taking a couple of backward paces.

'Hold it, Malloy!' In his hand was Malloy's sidearm.

Outwardly impassive for a moment, Malloy inwardly cursed himself. How goddamned stupid! Euston must be on Kane's payroll. Beyond Euston he saw the branches of the birches stir. Malloy's anger erupted.

'You no-good sonovabitch! You're gonna

hang for this, Euston.'

Euston snickered. 'Yeah, sure I am, Malloy.' Euston turned his head slightly. 'OK! I got what you want,' he shouted.

From within the thick stand of trees there came the rustling of leaves, and the breaking of twigs. A few moments later Bart Kane appeared astride his big roan, reaching up with one hand to push aside the last of the low branches. When Kane was clear, another rider to his right, unknown to Malloy, burst from the trees, leading a paint which Malloy recognized as belonging to Euston.

He eyed the distance between himself and Euston.

'You reach fer that knife, Malloy, an' I'm gonna shoot,' Euston said. He took a further couple of paces back as Kane reined in.

'Have to hand it to you, Malloy. You sure take a mite catchin',' Kane said. 'I just spent a whole goddamned night out here, waitin' for you.' Kane's eyes gleamed with triumph. 'Marcus is sure het up. Even cussin' me. Wants your blood real bad.'

Taking care to stay some distance from Malloy, Kane swung down from his saddle and pulled out his sidearm.

'Bring that cannon over, Euston. Then take the knife off Malloy.'

Euston didn't move. 'I done enough, Bart. I'm waitin' for my money.'

'Do as I godamned tell you! You get your money when Malloy ain't gotta a chance of breakin' free.'

Euston hesitated, and for an instant Malloy thought that the difference between the two men might give him a chance. Then Euston relaxed.

'Sure, Bart, that's the way you want it.'

He went around Kane's horse keeping well clear of crossing any firing-line and handed over the Peacemaker. Then he circled behind Malloy until he was close behind him. Malloy remained still as he felt Euston's hand slide into his vest pocket and pull out his throwing-knife. The deputy came back into his view as he rounded Kane's horse and handed over the knife to Bart.

Without turning his head, Kane shouted an order to the rider behind him.

'Jake! Give Euston his money and his horse.'

As Jake approached, Euston turned to Malloy.

'It ain't what I wanted, Malloy, but Masonville's finished, an' a man's gotta look out for hisself.'

'You're still gonna hang!'

Euston shrugged. 'Mebbe. But you ain't gonna be around to see it.'

He turned and took his reins and the bag of jingling coins from Jake who had joined them with the paint.

'I'm outta this territory, Kane,' Euston said. 'Now you got only Campbell between you an' Masonville.'

He pulled the head of his paint around and dug his spurs into the sides of his horse, heading for the trail. Kane continued to keep his eyes on Malloy. What was Kane waiting for? More men to appear?

Then Kane spoke. 'OK, Jake. Gimme that Spencer.'

The rider took his rifle from its scabbard and passed it across to Kane who brought it up to his shoulder. Malloy's eyes were transfixed by Kane's actions. Even at this short range Kane was taking care to squeeze the trigger rather than snatching at it. There was the ear-hammering crack of the long-gun and Malloy turned his head to see Euston topple from his saddle, hit the ground like a sack of oats, and lie still.

'Always did hate a four-flusher, Malloy,' Kane said. 'Go get the money, Jake, and Malloy can ride Euston's paint back to the Creek.'

'Hows about the palomino? Mighty nice-lookin' horseflesh.'

Jake's voice rasped as if his throat had once been wounded. He pointed towards where the horse had wandered off, his head down, nibbling the lush grass.

'Horse'll find its way back to Mason,' Kane said. 'Give the sodbusters another scare. Folks might even come lookin' for Malloy afore Euston is wolf-meat.'

'You're takin' a big chance, Kane, you gonna haul me back to the fort,' Malloy said.

Kane made a big show of looking at the Peacemaker in his hand and Malloy's empty holster.

'Oh, yeah? An' how you reckon on that, Malloy?'

'How about I do a deal with Marcus? I'm as fast as you, and I got more brains. You'll maybe end up swinging in the wind.'

Kane snickered. 'Gotta hand it to you, Malloy. I'd hate to play poker with you. You ain't gonna give in easy.' He stepped back, keeping the Peacemaker aimed at Malloy. 'Even if you was bein' straight you ain't gotta chance. You shouldna stole them papers. I ain't seen Marcus riled up like this for a long time.'

Kane heaved himself into his saddle as Jake approached with the paint.

'I'm gonna tell you, Malloy, what you're ridin' into. Soon as Marcus gets back he's gonna let our half-breed Comanche show what he got taught. You gotta few days to think on that. Then me an' Marcus, we're gonna watch the action.'

He held up Malloy's Peacemaker. 'Now get on that paint.'

CHAPTER TEN

Malloy opened his eyes when he heard the long iron key rattle in the lock. The cell door creaked open and the stooped old jailer appeared in the doorway. In his hands were a platter of beans and a chunk of rough bread, the same as he'd carried into Malloy at daybreak for the last five days.

The old man had spoken with Malloy only on that first day. Then he'd checked the shackle around Malloy's wrist before handing him the wooden platter and a spoon.

'You can maybe take this key off me,' he'd said. 'I ain't so young as I used to be.' He'd laughed humourlessly, showing bare gums. 'Then what you gonna do? You ain't gotta chance o' breakin' outta the fort. Try anythin' loco, an' you ain't gonna even get to the privy.'

The old man could have saved his breath. When Bart's gunnies had held him down and Bart had locked the shackle Malloy knew there was no chance of breaking out. He'd seen this type of shackle a hundred times before, guessing it had been left behind when the Army quit the fort.

Now the old man shuffled across the cell and stood in front of Malloy. Wordlessly, Malloy raised his right hand for the old man to inspect the shackle. Satisfied, the old man took from the pocket of his bib overall a wooden spoon and handed it with the platter to Malloy.

After Malloy had finished his chow both platter and spoon would be taken away. If his routine was followed, the old man would then bring him coffee in a wooden mug.

Later, he would return with one of Bart's men carrying a sidearm while Malloy used the open channel at the back of the cell. Neither man would speak to the other or to Malloy while in the cell. So Malloy looked up quickly from his plate of beans when the old man broke the silence.

'You a religious man?'

Malloy looked into the old man's rheumy eyes. What sort of question was that?

'Same as most men, I guess.'

'I ain't s'posed to tell you but you best know. Mr Marcus gets back tomorrow noon. You might wanna do some thinkin' afore then.'

Did pity show in the old man's eyes for

an instant?

'Thanks, ol'-timer. I'm obliged.'

The old man stared down at him for a few moments, then without another word turned and shuffled out of the cell, locking the door behind him.

Malloy continued to raise the wooden spoon, carrying the beans to his mouth and chewing them without any awareness of their taste. Bart believed his brother's fury was due to Malloy taking important papers from Strawberry Jack. Malloy knew differently. Stopping the stage hold-up was just luck. Marcus could blame Bart for the Peters girl. The train business was different. Marcus had been humiliated. If news of that had gotten to his band of gunslingers, men like the Mex in the saloon, Mendoza, and the rest of the gun sharks might start thinking they were working for the wrong man.

Marcus would arrive the following day maybe hoping to see Malloy begging for his life. Was Bart's threat of the half-breed the talk of a crazy man, too wary of his brother's rage to kill Malloy himself? Malloy had seen the half-breed standing around when Bart and Jake had brought him into the fort. His chest tightened with pain.

The old man was right. He'd got some

thinking to do. As he finished the beans, his hand dropped to the notch in his boot. Maybe the Kanes would have him thrown into the ground before one of their trail-trash stole his boots.

His fingers pushed against the notch, feeling the pressure against his shin. At least for a few weeks he'd known Beth Blackwell. Since he'd seen her that first time he'd thought her a fine lady. Now he knew she was a brave one. He'd learned, both down on the Border and in the Army, there were different types of bravery. An unmarried woman training to be a doctor, alone amongst so many men, must have showed real courage.

Most likely Beth would never know how he died, but now he had to show his own courage. At Dry Wood Creek, and down on the Border this past year, he'd had the chance to fight, his life in his own hands. There'd be no chance tomorrow. Malloy stared, unseeing, across at the wall of his cell. Summoning final courage would be the last gift he could grant Beth. Keeping the image of her face in his mind would stop him falling apart in the face of whatever Marcus intended for him.

He looked towards the door as the muffled

sound of raised voices and angry shouts broke out somewhere beyond his cell.

'I'm tellin' you, Bart. I gotta see him with my own eyes!'

What was going on? Malloy heard the steps halt beyond the door.

'You stupid sonovabitch!' Bart sounded as mad as a cornered rattler. 'You think I don't know Malloy! I got the bastard shackled in the cell waitin' for Marcus.'

The other's voice remained even.

'Afore Mr Marcus leaves Cheyenne he wants to be sure. You ain't done so well of late, Bart...'

There was the sound of a fist hitting flesh as the speaker was cut off in mid-sentence. There was a scuffling of feet and then a loud thump against the door.

'That ain't changin' anythin', Bart.' The voice, still defiant, was low down outside the door and Malloy guessed that the speaker had been knocked down and was scrambling to his feet. 'Mr Marcus says I gotta see who you got and report back to him.'

'For two cents I'd shoot you down right now!' Bart hollered. 'How do I know you ain't some sort of spy?'

'Mr Marcus thought o' that. Here, Bart, he gave me this to show you.'

There was a pause while Malloy guessed Bart was examining something. Then Bart spoke, his voice more even.

'You'da been a damned sight smarter if you'd shown me this before. I guess you're OK. Open the door, old man.'

The shuffling of the old man's steps halted beyond the door, and the key rattled in the lock. Slowly the door opened. Beyond the jailer Malloy saw Bart and the gunman, Jake. Beyond them, out of sight of Malloy, the other man spoke.

'You both got sidearms an' I ain't. If that's Malloy in there you gotta go in first.'

'You lily-livered whelp! Malloy's shackled. He ain't gonna cause trouble.'

'Mr Marcus said...'

'Fer crissakes!' Bart exploded. 'Jake, get in there! Stand by Malloy, an' this chicken-heart ain't gonna get himself hurt!'

Malloy sat up on his bunk, squaring his shoulders. He wasn't about to give Bart or Marcus's messenger the notion he was a beaten man. But it was plain that Marcus didn't trust Bart any longer. If only he'd managed to drive a wedge between the Kane brothers before now, maybe he could have made something out of it. Maybe he should have told more folks about the train instead of keeping quiet on account of the money going to the new horses. He grunted aloud. Too late, anyways, to think about that.

He stared at Jake as the gunman entered the cell and moved to Malloy's right, standing so that the gun on his hip was beyond Malloy's reach.

Bart followed him in the cell to stand maybe six feet from Malloy, a leer on his face.

'You ain't lookin' too good, Malloy.' He sniffed the air deliberately. 'Don't smell too good, neither. Ain't that right, Jake?' Then without taking his eyes off Malloy he called out. 'C'mon in, chicken-liver. So's you can tell my brother what I got for him.'

'Sure, Bart. I hope to hell it's Malloy, an' I can be on my way.'

There was the sound of scuffling feet and from the shadows behind Bart, who remained leering at Malloy, Jed Miller stepped into the cell.

'Jake!' said Malloy.

Instinctively, the gunman's gaze shifted from Jed to Malloy. He died in that instant. The flat throwing-knife thrown by Jed buried up to the hilt in his throat. Blood sprayed as his knees buckled and he crumpled to the floor within Malloy's reach.

Bart's eyes popped. 'What the hell...?'

Then his mouth closed like a rat-trap as the derringer pulled by Jed from beneath his vest screwed into his temple.

'You move your mouth or your hands, Bart, an' you're dead.'

'Jed! The old man!' Malloy said urgently, snatching the sidearm off Jake's body.

'Out cold.' Jed eased the short-gun from Bart's gunbelt.

'Jes lookit here!' he said, staring down at Malloy's Peacemaker. 'You ain't only a murderin' rattlesnake, Kane, you're also a low-down thief!'

'He's got the shackle key, Jed!'

Kane spat in Malloy's direction. 'You try an' find it!'

'Bust his knee, Jed, but no blood! We're gonna need him.'

'Hold on, you crazy bastards! Roun' my neck.'

Jed tore at Kane's shirt, pulling over his head the black rawhide cord holding the key. He threw it across the cell to Malloy who quickly unlocked the shackle.

'You got horses, Jed? Or we gonna steal 'em?'

'I got somethin' better. A wagon inside the gates. But how the hell we gonna get out?'

Malloy handed the sidearm he'd taken

158

from Jake's body to Jed, exchanging it for his own Peacemaker. The heavy weapon felt comfortable in his hand as he slid it into the empty holster on his hip.

'This sidewinder's gonna lead the way. He opens his mouth afore we reach the wagon, we kill him an' take our chances.'

Malloy snatched Kane's hat, put it on his own head and pulled it low over his eyes.

'Gimme the derringer, Jed,' he said.

He forced the little sidearm against the base of Kane's spine.

'I once saw a poor critter of a Mex rustler with a little slug in his spine. Took two days to die and for his last eight hours he was screamin' for someone to shoot him. Tol' us all we wanted to know.' He screwed the barrel harder against Kane. 'You gonna give us any trouble?'

Kane shook his head.

'No trouble, Malloy.'

Malloy pushed him forward.

'Get goin'. An' remember, anyone asks, we're takin' a wagon ride into the Creek.'

The three men moved together out of the cell, Malloy holding Kane back for a few moments while Jed dragged the unconscious old man into the cell and closed the door. Ahead of them a flight of stone steps led up to a long corridor at ground level. From when he was brought here some six days before Malloy recalled there was a door at the end wall.

'Critter mannin' the gate tol' me to bring the wagon round this side of the fort,' Jed explained. 'The gunnies are bunkin' on the other side, far as I could tell.'

Malloy prodded Kane forward again.

'You jes' might get to live today,' he said.

They went up the stairs slowly, pausing at the top step to listen for anyone moving. There was no sound and Malloy kept close behind Kane as they stepped into the corridor. Two minutes later Jed was easing open the door set in the rough wooden timbers and looking out into the morning light.

'Coupla men over on the far side takin' water from the well. They ain't gonna bother us,' he reported to Malloy.

Malloy spoke softly close to Kane's ear.

'I'll say it once, Kane. You'll get up front with Jed. I'll be in the wagon. You make any signal, make any move that I ain't comfortable with and I'm gonna put a bullet in your spine. You got that?'

Kane nodded. 'I tol' you, Malloy. No trouble.'

Malloy thrust Kane's hat back into his

hand, and signalled Jed to take care of Kane. Scanning the open area of the fort, he waited until the two men had turned towards the old sutler's store before slipping through the doorway and heaving himself into the back of the wagon. Beneath the flax of the wagon's cover the boards were warm against him as he lay at full stretch. He was just able to see the gate, barred as it would have been during the Army's time. A moment later his view was obscured as Kane and Jed took their places. Stretching out his arm, Malloy held the barrel of his Peacemaker hard against Kane.

Jed flicked the reins and the wagon rumbled forward. If there was going to be trouble it would be at the gate. Malloy heard Jed call to the horse and the wagon came to a halt. Footsteps approached the wagon. They were at the gate.

'Mornin', Bart. You're sure up an' about this day.'

There was a long silence, and Malloy rammed his sidearm into Kane's back.

'Tell him to close up after,' he said softly.

'Ain't even sure I'm awake, Frank. Me an' this feller goin' down the Creek, pick up some stuff. You better close up after we're gone.'

'Sure, Bart. Just hold on there.'

There was a banging of stout timbers against each other as the sentry unbarred the gate. With a squeal of iron hinges Malloy heard the heavy gate being pushed open.

'OK, Bart. Have a couple o' beers for me,' Frank shouted, a little out of breath.

An order from Jed and a flick of the reins in his hand, and the wagon rolled forward, heading for the bend in the trail that led to Silver Creek. Behind them Malloy heard the sound of timbers as the gate was closed.

The wagon rounded the bend and Jed urged the horse into a trot. Malloy scrambled to his feet. He reversed the Peacemaker and brought the butt crashing down on to Kane's head. As Kane slumped forward Malloy threw his arm around Kane's neck and dragged him back into the body of the wagon. He holstered his sidearm, picked up a length of cord from the bottom of the wagon and secured Kane's hands and ankles. Then he climbed to the front of the wagon alongside Jed.

'Trail divides three ways about a mile ahead,' explained Jed. 'One goes to Silver Creek; there's a second trail called Wolf Creek but that's been out of use since the old Injun gave up runnin' the raft 'cross the river.

We'd best take the regular trail.' Jed flicked the reins again urging the horse forward.

They'd gone maybe a mile, Malloy checking at regular intervals that no riders were following them, when Jed broke the silence. He turned to Malloy, a grin across his face.

'What you reckon, Mr Malloy? You thinkin' I was damned good back there?'

'Stop callin' me mister. Makes me feel old.' Malloy looked sideways at the young man whose gaze was fixed ahead again. How could he have questioned Jed's ability to go up against the Kanes? One thing still puzzled him, though.

'Tell me, Jed. What the hell convinced this critter back here you came from Marcus?'

If possible, Jed's grin grew wider.

'You remember tellin' me about the train, guessin' Marcus would keep his mouth shut.'

'Sure, an' I reckon I was right.'

'I'm damned glad you were.' Jed thrust a hand into his vest pocket, to hold up Marcus Kane's Albert chain and watch. 'Cassidy said he'd give me hell if I didn't bring this back.'

CHAPTER ELEVEN

Malloy stepped out of Campbell's office, refreshed after the sleep he'd snatched in the spare bunk at the back of the jail. He closed the door behind him, shutting off the sounds of Campbell hollering at Bart Kane that there'd be no chow if he didn't quit cussing.

Campbell, convinced his deputy had been killed by Caleb Wood, had been rattled when he'd learned of Euston's treachery.

'Tol' him everythin'. Shoulda kept my mouth shut,' he said. But he'd recovered quickly. 'I'll talk with Cap'n Joe. Maybe recruit one of his Volunteers.'

Malloy looked up and down Main Street. With Bart Kane in the cage it was wise to stay alert. Reassured, he went down the steps, raising a finger to his new Stetson as a young woman carrying a basket greeted him, her eyes curious.

As he headed for Stockin's bank he was aware of other townsfolk watching his progress. Some greeted him cheerfully, and more than a few wished him well, congratulating him on his escape. The news had spread fast, no doubt helped by Jed still whooping and hollering about the events at the fort. Jed had the right, Malloy reckoned, to whoop and holler as much as he wanted. He recalled wondering if Jed had the guts to go up against the Kanes. Best if Jed never knew he'd thought like that.

As he made his way along Main Street he guessed that not all the townsfolk were pleased at his reappearance. Their expressions were wary, and twice Malloy overhead uneasy mutterings about Bart Kane in Campbell's jail. Maybe one or two whose glances lingered on his Peacemaker were on Marcus Kane's payroll. He blew out air from between pursed lips. He was just plain jumpy after being held in the fort.

The folks around him were honest decent townsfolk who mostly looked with suspicion at all men who wore guns, save for their local sheriff. Law and order were rapidly moving West and the days of every man toting sidearms were past. One day this Territory would become a State of the Union. But that was going to take time. The townsfolk had to understand that Marcus Kane would control their lives if ever he took over Masonville.

His thoughts switched rapidly as he noticed Beth's buggy tied to a hitching-post. What had brought her into town this early?

He stepped up to the boardwalk and pushed open the door of the bank. Behind the counter was a young woman he vaguely recognized. He guessed she'd taken the place of the dead clerk. She appeared to be no older than the Peters girl. What was that remark of Beth's? Something about the century moving on? Maybe this young woman was another sign of that.

'Mornin' ma'am. I'm told Mr Stockin would...'

He was interrupted by a door at the rear of the bank opening and Stockin greeting him with an outstretched hand.

'I'm mighty glad to see you alive, Mr Malloy.' The banker, beaming with pleasure, shook his hand vigorously. 'Please step this way.'

Puzzled by what was required of him, Malloy followed Stockin into his private office. Stepping through the door he was surprised to see Beth sitting opposite Stockin's desk. She hadn't said anything about this meeting when he'd seen her briefly the previous evening.

She looked up at him.

'Mr Stockin asked me to come in. I'm as much in the dark as you are.'

'Take a seat, Mr Malloy.' Stockin lowered his bulk into the stout oak chair behind the desk. 'I apologize for the secrecy but what I have to tell you could affect the whole future of the town.' He sighed heavily. 'With Abraham gone...' His voice trailed away, as he picked up papers from his desk and cleared his throat.

'I've the major's will here, which he made a year or so ago. He did make one small addition only a few days before he died. Although I can tell you, Beth, he made no changes of importance where you're concerned.'

Malloy glanced at Beth and saw her eyes widen in surprise.

'I'm in Abraham's will?' Beth said. 'Surely his family or any kin of Mrs Walker have their claims.'

Stockin shook his head.

'All of Mrs Walker's kinfolk died during the War. The Walkers' only child, a son, died many years ago.'

The banker glanced down at his papers as if to remind himself of what they contained. 'Abraham was always quite clear what he wanted. I've already spoken with Henry.

He's been left enough to marry Missy and buy his own place.'

Malloy knew Missy from seeing her at Beth's house, although he hadn't known that Henry and she were close. Something else he didn't know. Why was he here? Was he meant to support Beth? Surely the major hadn't made any bequests to him after so short an acquaintance.

Stockin cleared his throat again.

'Aside from those funds for Henry and one further small bequest, Beth, the entire estate goes to you.'

Malloy heard Beth gasp with shock. He turned to see her open-mouthed, gazing at the banker.

'You're now a very rich woman, no matter what happens here in Masonville,' Stockin said.

Malloy glanced at Beth who still appeared shocked into silence, before he spoke.

'Mr Stockin, this might be none of my business but what d'you mean by that?'

Stockin shifted in his chair.

'Marcus Kane has made several attempts to buy the big house and all its land. Abraham knew that if he sold, it would be delivering the town into Kane's hands. The town's maybe young but folks here have invested their money and ten years of their lives. Abraham was not about to let Kane take that away.' Stockin sighed heavily. 'But that was before Abraham went to his grave.'

He shuffled his papers, a gloomy expression marking his face, and glanced down again at the top page before looking up again at Beth.

'Abraham wanted to give you the chance of returning to Boston and becoming the great surgeon he and your father always believed you could be. Before your father died he explained to Abraham the huge obstacles you would face.' Stockin's gloom lifted and he smiled. 'Abraham had a realistic view of money and Boston society.'

Beth's face had reddened.

'This is all so sudden,' she said. 'I can't say anything yet.'

Stockin nodded. 'Of course. There's no hurry.' He turned in his seat to face Malloy. 'The major was very careful how he worded your bequest, Mr Malloy.'

Malloy knew he must have looked surprised. Walker hadn't said anything to him about this. Beth had been left everything, so what had Walker written in his will?

Stockin looked down at his papers as if to recall the exact words.

'If at the time of Abraham's death you were living permanently more than twenty-five miles from the big house you were to receive nothing. If you lived less than twenty-five miles you were to be given the major's Cavalry sword,' he said.

Malloy sat still. Like Beth, there was nothing he could say. Why him? Why not Captain Joe of the Volunteers, for example? The captain was an old Cavalryman. He, Malloy, was just a passing stranger. True, he'd told the major he'd help with the Concord but the major was dead before the first stage run.

'You mind tellin' me when the major wrote this about his sword?'

'The day he showed you the Concord. He rode in after you'd left town.'

Then Malloy remembered. Was that what Walker was trying to say as he lay dying? 'Will you take the sword?' It made sense.

Stockin shuffled his papers on his desk.

'There'll be more papers for Beth to sign, of course, but that's as far as we need to go today.'

The two men stood as Beth got up from her chair. Stockin moved around his desk to open the door, and escorted them around the counter to the door. Malloy waited while

Beth exchanged farewells with both the young woman and Stockin before promising that she would return the following day. Then she and Malloy stepped out into the sunlight.

Malloy waited until Stockin had closed the door behind them before speaking.

'I guess we need to talk,' he said.

'Yes,' Beth said, a distant look in her blue eyes.

'How about a buggy ride?'

This time she turned to him and looked up at him when she spoke. Concern showed in her eyes.

'Is it safe?'

'We'll not go far,' he said. 'Just out to the brook.'

A few minutes later they were heading in the direction of the meadow that lay about half a mile from the edge of town and maybe 500 yards from the trail heading east. Malloy, occupied by his thoughts, held the pony on a loose rein, allowing the animal to proceed at its own pace. Alongside Malloy, Beth too was silent. Malloy contented himself with scanning the horizon, watching the rain clouds scud over the hills to the south, and being glad he was alive and taking a buggy ride with this pretty and clever young woman.

He turned the pony off the trail, the buggy wheels pushing aside the lush grass towards the brook until he reined in a dozen yards from the water. Ripples showed as fish rose for flies. Malloy hooked the reins over the board, leaned back, and took a deep breath.

'Sure is great country,' he said.

'It's beautiful,' Beth said. She was silent for a few moments. 'When Abraham first saw this land he wrote my father that he'd found paradise. He urged my father to join him and help build a new life for people after the War.'

Malloy nodded. 'I ain't sure the townsfolk know how much they owed the major. I reckon without him Marcus Kane would own Masonville by now.' He paused, thinking about what Stockin had told them. 'Maybe the major guessed what might happen and made his plans.'

'I'm not sure I understand.'

'Sure he had hopes of you becoming a great doctor. Maybe even a mite more hope than he had for the future of the town. But he was too big a man to corral you. So he's handed you the choice. Stay here or go back East.'

Beth was silent for a few moments.

'I've family back in Boston and I plan to

172

visit them sometime. But I shall always return.'

Malloy studied her face. 'To the big house?'

She nodded vigorously. 'Where else? The people of this town need me.'

'Even if Marcus Kane takes over the town?'

'They'll need me in the big house even more if that happens.'

'I guess they will,' Malloy said soberly.

Beth placed a hand on his arm. 'You also have a choice. This isn't your town.'

Malloy shook his head. 'Marcus Kane has set out to kill me. I can't walk away from that.' His mouth set firm. 'That's why the major left me his sword, I reckon. One Cavalryman reminding another of what's needed to be done.'

For a moment Malloy's face remained grim, then he relaxed and grinned down at Beth's upturned face.

'Besides, this rib o' mine ain't healed fully yet, and you might wanna take another look.'

Beth's face grew pink.

'John Malloy! I'm a doctor!' She stopped abruptly as they heard the sounds of galloping hoofs. They both swung around to

173

watch the horseman bent low in his saddle heading into town.

Malloy snatched up the reins, all pleasant talk forgotten.

'That's the Mexican barman from the Creek. Looks like there's somethin' going on I need to know about!'

He flicked the pony's back urging the animal into a fast trot. Beth held on to Malloy's arm as the buggy bounced along, its wheels scything through the grass of the meadow until they bumped on to the small stones and packed earth of the trail. The Mexican was now well ahead of them, his mount reaching the softer ground of Main Street.

Malloy urged the pony on to greater speed in time to see the Mexican rein in outside Campbell's office. Barely waiting to secure his horse at the hitching-post the Mexican hurried up the steps and entered the sheriff's office. Was this part of some crazy plan to break Bart out of Campbell's jail? As Malloy was dismissing the notion from his mind he saw the Mexican reappear on the boardwalk. A moment later he came galloping past them heading out of town.

Malloy slowed the pony as they drew level with Campbell's office.

'That was danged quick! Here, Beth. Take

these. I'm gonna see the sheriff.'

He passed over the reins, and before Beth could reply, he jumped from the moving buggy, took the steps to the boardwalk two at a time and flung open the door to Campbell's office.

'What the hell was all that about?'

Then he saw Campbell's face. The sheriff sat still behind his desk looking towards Malloy, his focus somewhere distant beyond Malloy's shoulder. Malloy frowned. Was the sheriff wounded?

'You OK, Campbell?'

The sheriff twitched his shoulders, appearing to look at Malloy for the first time since he'd opened the door. Confusion troubled the older man's eyes. Malloy had seen that look before in the eyes of young Cavalrymen when Johnny Reb opened up with cannons.

'They're comin' in tomorrow,' Campbell said dully. 'Marcus Kane an' his gunnies will be here at noon to pick up Bart. If I don't give up Bart they'll break him out.' Campbell lowered his head, holding one hand against his forehead.

Malloy said nothing. Instead he walked across to the stove and peered into the metal pot. Then he took down a mug and poured himself a measure of the thick black liquid.

He took a sip and looked back at Campbell.

'OK, let Kane have his brother.'

Campbell jerked up in his chair, his eyes clearing.

'Are you loco? I reckon Bart Kane's a murdering sonovabitch, but I ain't judge and jury. He's gonna stand trial!'

A faint smile flickered around Malloy's lips.

'OK, we got that outta the way.' He took another sip from the steaming mug. 'You gotta Bible in that desk someplace?'

'Sure.'

'Then mebbe you could find me a badge to go with it. Seems like you're gonna need all the help you can get.'

CHAPTER TWELVE

Malloy glanced up at the wall above Campbell's head. The morning sunshine was throwing shadows across the clock face.

'Maybe a coupla hours afore Kane shows. Let's see what we got. You first, Sheriff.'

Campbell's mouth twisted with bitter humour.

'Folks ain't exactly rushin' to give a hand. But it ain't all bad. I can count on six, an' four of 'em fought in the War.' Again his mouth twisted. 'Tho' they did wear butternut brown.'

'Shame we ain't gotta regiment of Johnny Rebs,' said Jed. 'I ain't done so good. Only got a coupla Haines' fellers from the livery. Tol' me I was righteous to stand agin evil, an' they'd stand with me.' Jed's face flushed. 'Most folks looked at my badge and tol' me I dunno dung from wild honey.'

'Forget it, Jed. They ain't caught up with you yet,' said Malloy. 'You did better than me, I reckon. Beth hadn't been with me I ain't sure any folk woulda turned out.

Anyways, I got ten with one more to see.'

He looked across at Henry whose faded shirt showed the insignia of the Fifty-fourth Massachusetts Volunteers.

'I got three come up from the south. Kinfolk of Missy,' Henry said. 'We all served under the major and Colonel Shaw. They come this far, got their freedom, they're gonna fight like hellcats if needs be.'

'A coupla dozen an' Cap'n Joe and his men,' Malloy said slowly. 'You got any thoughts, Sheriff?'

Campbell looked at each of the three men before looking back at Malloy.

'I'm thinkin' that afore the Kanes arrived I pulled drunken cowboys outta the saloon and collected taxes. I've a notion you done this before. I ain't too proud to listen.'

Malloy held Campbell's gaze for a moment, and then nodded.

'OK, when we done here get hold of Bridge an' tell him we need everything in his back cupboard, an' as much ammo he's got. He knows he'll get his money.' He thought for a moment. 'We still got any hands in town from the old mine?'

'My old man was with the company,' Jed said. 'Coupla old-timers he worked with are still in town.'

178

'Round 'em up. Tell 'em they ain't gonna get shot at, but this is what we need.' Malloy quickly outlined what he wanted. When he'd finished Jed asked a couple of questions, and after hearing Malloy's answers, nodded his head.

'Got it,' he said.

'You better get goin'.'

Campbell looked across his office as the door closed on Jed.

'I'm gonna have to watch myself. That boy's gonna be after my job next year.' His smile faded. 'That's if we come outta this,' he added sombrely.

Malloy turned to Henry.

'Sheriff'll give you a list of all the folks we got. You get 'em all at the east end of town by eleven o'clock. I'll tell 'em then what we're gonna do. First I gotta see Cap'n Joe and George in the saloon.'

He turned over an idea in his mind. 'Bend in the trail on the east side means we ain't gonna be lookin' into the sun if we face 'em at the edge of town. I guess the three of us know what we're takin' on. So do the Southern boys, I reckon. But we're gonna have to look out for the townsfolk best we can.' He glanced up at the clock. 'Time we were movin'.'

179

Half an hour later Malloy stepped up from Main Street on to the boardwalk. Save for Campbell and Bridge carrying long-guns across their outstretched arms, the street was deserted. The townsfolk were keeping well out of the way. If Bart Kane hadn't been in Campbell's jail then there wouldn't be all this trouble, four of the storekeepers had told Malloy the previous evening. He couldn't think badly of them. Lots of folks felt the same, he reckoned.

He'd detected similar doubts ten minutes before when he'd been with Captain Joe. A couple of his Volunteers looked mighty sick they'd ever taken bounty money from Masonville. When Captain Joe had suggested that not all the Volunteers muster with the townsfolk Malloy had thought for a moment the old soldier had also spotted them. But when he'd explained what he was thinking, Malloy saw what he was driving at.

'Get the best four over to Bridge. Tell Campbell what we got in mind,' he'd told Captain Joe.

Now Malloy had only George to see. He pushed through the batwing doors and entered the saloon. The place was empty save for George behind the bar polishing a glass. Maybe the hurdy-gurdy girls were

180

upstairs wondering who they'd be dancing with tonight. The saloonkeeper looked up as Malloy approached the bar.

'What you reckonin', George?' Malloy asked.

The saloonkeeper looked up with a nervous smile.

'Mr Malloy, I ain't never had much to do with firearms, an' I ain't too smart on a horse. But I got this.' He dropped his hand below the bar and pulled out an ancient shotgun, its barrel sawn short. 'Reckon this ol' scatter-gun might see off one or two of those varmints.'

'Reckon you could be right, George. I'm obliged to you. Henry'll be 'round to tell you what's happenin'.' He began to turn away but George held up his hand. 'Got somethin' else for you, Mr Malloy. Set you up for noontime real good.'

As Malloy paused, George turned and picked up a china mug. He placed it on the bar and half-filled it with coffee from a metal pot.

'You're right, George,' Malloy said. Since hearing of Marcus Kane coming into Masonville it seemed as if he'd done nothing but talk. His throat was beginning to rasp.

'Hold on, Mr Malloy,' George said as

Malloy reached for the mug.

Again George reached below the bar but this time brought up a small metal jug in one hand and a bottle with the other. He poured cream from the jug on to the hot black liquid, and then uncorked the bottle.

'Fine French brandy, Mr Malloy,' he said proudly. 'Drummer from down South left it for his gaming-debt. Showed me what to do.' George poured a generous measure of the spirit into the creamy coffee.

Malloy looked down at the mug for a long moment, his mind suddenly full of the picture of a tall, graceful woman. A woman, still beautiful, whose fine breeding overcame her years. He remembered her at the table, her one remaining servant from the old country pouring cream from a silver jug. The picture in Malloy's mind seemed covered with gauze, its place in a world that he'd long since left behind.

'I'm tellin' you, George, I ain't seen anyone do that for a long, long, time,' he said slowly.

Malloy lifted the mug and drank half its contents in one gulp, the liquid soothing his throat before reaching his stomach where it spread a warm glow. He lowered the mug to the bar, running his tongue around his lips, tasting the last of the sweetness.

'Sure beats black coffee!'

Seeing George looking past him towards the batwing doors, he turned.

'Reckon Doc Blackwell's out there waitin', Mr Malloy.'

Malloy turned to catch a glimpse of Beth as she moved away from the entrance to the saloon. What was she doing out on Main Street? He'd told her to stay out of sight. He strode over to the entrance, his boots disturbing the sawdust on the boarded floor, and pushed through the doors. Beth was a few yards along the boardwalk.

'Thought we'd agreed you were stayin' at home,' he said as she turned to face him.

'I've thought more about it. I'm not hiding away because Marcus Kane is threatening the town.' Her lips set in a determined line. 'If the town council gives way to him then the people of this town will need me even more.'

'Beth, three of the council are gonna be there at noon. They gave you their word.'

'Yes, so it's important I'm there, too.'

Malloy frowned. Why the hell couldn't some women just stay told? Some of these fancy notions coming from back East were just making life damned difficult. There was no way he was going to allow Beth to be

183

there at noon. Marcus Kane was no longer taking his time to gain control of the town. He'd most likely offered a large reward to the man who shot his way to Campbell's office. The trail-trash who rode for Kane wouldn't care who stood before them.

'A lotta good folks could get killed today,' he said.

She nodded, her face set firm.

'I know that. I've spoken with Henry. I shall set up a place in the bank to take care of any wounded. Missy knows what's needed, and Lucy from the bank will help.'

Malloy suddenly remembered where he'd seen Lucy before. Beth sure took his breath away sometimes.

'She that saloon gal you took care of?'

'Was a saloon girl,' she corrected. 'Henry says she's faster at figures than he is.' The smile which had appeared for an instant, faded away. 'You take care at noon, John Malloy,' she said. She held his gaze for a few moments then turned away, heading for her buggy.

Malloy didn't move, his eyes following her progress along the boardwalk.

Campbell stood up in his stirrups so the assembled line of riders could see and hear him clearly.

'Afore Kane an' his men ride in I wanna tell you a coupla things. Coupla days ago young Jed Miller did somethin' over at the fort none of us could match. That's why he's gotta badge. Henry here, fought alongside Major Walker in the War, an' that should be good enough for everyone. We all want to get through this. So if me an' Cap'n Joe can listen to Mr Malloy today, then I'm danged sure all o' you can.'

The sheriff lowered himself back into the saddle and looked around at Malloy, who turned his palomino's head so he faced the assembled riders. The faces of the men were tense, most with determination, some showing signs of nervousness. A couple of men close to Malloy, homesteaders who'd been tricked out of their land, stared back at him with pale faces, their hands trembling slightly on their reins.

Malloy reckoned that in their own way they were as brave as the four Southerners who sat relaxed on their mounts, their Winchesters supplied by Bridge already. unsheathed from their leather scabbards.

Malloy looked straight at the homesteaders although he raised his voice to reach the whole line of riders.

'We're gonna meet Kane just outta town. That's where we're plannin' to turn 'em back. If shootin' starts, we got enough long-guns to take 'em on.' He turned his head to look along the line. 'The badges an' Cap'n Joe will be up front. I want the Southern boys either side of us an' ten yards back. Rest of you twenty yards behind 'em and strung across the trail.'

A voice called out. 'We coulda used more Volunteers.'

Cap'n Joe turned in the direction of the speaker.

'Don't you worry, Fred. They'll be here.'

Someone shouted from Malloy's right.

'What the hell do we do if Kane's men break through the lines?'

Then four badges, Cap'n Joe and the Southern boys will all be down, and you'll be on your own, thought Malloy. He wasn't about to say it. Instead, he held up an outstretched arm and pointed towards where the trail broke on to Main Street. Three elderly men were crossing back and forth laying a cord in the dust.

'Jed's old man's got enough powder to blow 'em to hell and back!'

One of the men from the South let out a whoop.

186

'Never thought I'd be damned glad to hear a Rebel yell,' a rider in an old blue shirt shouted, grinning sheepishly as he was both shouted down and cheered by the remainder of the riders.

'You might just hold 'em together,' Captain Joe muttered to Malloy.

The laughter died away and silence fell on the men as the distant sound of galloping horses reached their ears.

'They're comin' in,' shouted Malloy. 'No shootin', 'less I give the word.'

For a moment he watched the line of riders pull round the heads of their mounts and start moving to their positions. Then he turned his palomino and moved forward to ride into line. Captain Joe and Campbell rode to his left, Henry and Jed to his right. All five men halted level with the marker Malloy had placed on the side of the trail.

A stand of birches hid the approaching riders from Malloy. He'd know soon enough, he reasoned, but still he attempted to estimate the numbers of men from the sounds of galloping hoofs. No more than twenty, he guessed. If it came to a shoot-out, his greater numbers might just make up for the readiness of Kane's gunnies to use their weapons.

'About twenty, I reckon,' Captain Joe said tightly.

Malloy nodded grimly as the body of men led by Marcus Kane swept into view around the bend. The dust kicked up from the trail hung over them like a low brown cloud. Malloy heard Kane shout an order. The two columns of riders broke into a line heading directly towards them. At another shout maybe half the advancing riders drew their long-guns, riding with their reins in one hand.

'He's drilled 'em,' said Henry softly.

'But he ain't gonna start a war unless he has to,' said Captain Joe.

'I hope to hell you're right,' Jed said quietly. Then he sucked in air. 'Fer crissakes, they're comin' too close!'

The muscles in Malloy's shoulders tensed, but then relaxed as the advancing riders began to slow. Malloy turned in his saddle, and called to the men from the old Confederacy.

'We're gonna try an' parley,' he said. 'Remember what I said 'bout shootin'.'

Without waiting for a response he turned back to see Kane and his riders halt thirty yards away. Then at another given order the line advanced until Kane was no more than ten yards from Malloy's line.

Malloy glanced at the large stones he'd placed at the side of the trail.

'It's OK, he's not too close.'

He looked across the ten yards separating the lines. Kane's expression hadn't altered but some of his men were exchanging muttered remarks. Malloy guessed they were taken aback by the show of force. Maybe Kane had told them it was going to be easy work. Campbell and a couple of deputies, maybe. Malloy could see Kane struggling to control himself, fury working behind his cheeks, as he looked at the badges on the shirts of the men he faced.

'I know this ain't your idea, Campbell,' Kane called. 'Gimme my brother an' we all go home. That way nobody gets hurt.'

'Bart's gotta face a charge of murder,' Campbell called in reply. 'An' that's all there is to it.'

'You sorry sonovabitch! You got it all wrong!' Kane stood in his stirrups and shouted so all the riders ahead of him could hear. 'Listen to me! I swear on my mother's grave Bart didn't shoot Abe Walker.'

'Save your breath, Kane,' Malloy called. 'They know all that.'

Kane lowered himself slowly into his

saddle, staring hard across the divide at Malloy.

'What the hell d'you mean?'

'Will Euston bushwhacked Abraham Walker.'

If only he'd worked out faster the true meaning of the major's dying words, Malloy told himself, he'd have saved himself a whole heap of trouble. He saw that his answer had rattled Kane. At ten yards he could see the vein pulsing in Kane's temple.

'Then why you holdin' Bart?' Kane exploded.

'For backshootin' Euston,' Campbell replied. 'Euston was a double-dealer but he shoulda still gone to trial. That's what the law says.'

Kane ignored the sheriff, not shifting his gaze from Malloy.

'You been gettin' in my way since you came to Masonville. I've got twenty men here who know what they're doin'. You got maybe half a dozen and a bunch of dirt farmers. I give the word an' we're gonna bust Bart outta jail.'

Malloy glanced to his right, fixing on one of Kane's riders.

'Missouri!'

'Yo! Mr Malloy!'

'The ugly critter with the reservation hat to your right! If he moves his hands, shoot him!'

'Yo! Mr Malloy!'

'Now hold on...!'

'Shut your godamned mouth, Fletcher!' Kane shouted. He looked around at his line of riders, a sneer on his face. 'You all hear? Malloy's tryin' to throw a scare! Reckons we're a bunch of tenderfoots!'

A snicker of amusement ran along Kane's line of riders.

Malloy's expression didn't change.

'Henry!'

Without a word Henry took one hand from his reins and held it high. From his fingers fluttered a red neckerchief.

For a moment Kane looked puzzled. Again he turned his head left and then right to look along his line of riders.

'Now look at that!' he shouted. 'Buffalo soldier's got himself a fancy bandanna.'

From above and behind Malloy's line of riders came the ratcheting of metal on the roofs of the stores either side of Main Street as four Volunteers brought their Winchesters to bear above the heads of Malloy's line on to Kane.

Malloy spoke one word again. 'Henry!'

The neckerchief fluttered from Henry's fingers. There was the whipcrack of rifle fire and the dirt two yards ahead of Kane's horse spurted into the air as four Winchester slugs buried themselves into the ground. Kane's big grey and the horses close to him shied away, their hoofs pounding into the dirt.

'Sharpshooters got you in their sights, Kane!' Malloy shouted. 'You or your gunnies make one move an' you're dead men.'

Save for the skittering of horse's hoofs still unsettled after the rifle shots there was silence among the two groups of men as Malloy stared straight at Kane. He guessed Kane was working out the odds of remaining alive while giving his riders the order to start shooting. Malloy felt his chest tighten. One wrong move now by anyone and this could turn into a bloodbath.

Kane spat into the dirt.

'You better tell 'em to shoot, Malloy. 'Cos I'm gonna kill you if it takes the rest o' my days!'

Malloy felt his muscles relax.

'Tell your men to turn 'round and start ridin'. You don't move.'

For a few seconds Kane was still, looking beyond Malloy to the roofs of the Main Street stores. Without looking around Malloy knew the four men were well hidden.

'Do as he goddamn says,' Kane rasped.

One of Kane's riders shouted out:

'I ain't likin' this at all!'

For the first time Malloy saw the shadow of fear cross Kane's face, then Kane turned his head towards the rider.

'You wanna see nightfall, keep your mouth shut!'

Muttering among themselves, Kane's riders turned away, kicking their horses into action, and heading back along the trail towards Silver Creek. As Malloy watched them go he drew his Peacemaker for the first time. He kicked his horse forward to walk the ten yards to bring himself alongside Kane.

'You an' me we're gonna have to settle accounts some time,' Malloy said. 'But this ain't the day.' He leaned across, pulled Kane's sidearm from its holster and thrust it into the grey's saddle-bag. 'You try somethin' like this again, an' I reckon the whole town'll be out to meet you. US marshals are gonna start arrivin', you start a war.'

'Just you an' me, Malloy! That's what I'm lookin' for now! Then I'll make the goddamned townsfolk bend the knee!'

With a vicious heave on his grey's head, Kane pulled his horse's head around, and kicked his spurs cruelly into the animal's sides.

'I'll be back another day, Malloy!'

Aware of the ragged cheering behind him from the lines of riders, Malloy sat watching Kane riding after his men. From one of the men from the South came a yell that was followed by shouts of laughter.

Malloy glanced back to see that Henry and the three others hadn't moved, gazing past him in the direction of Kane's men. Malloy waited until Kane had disappeared around the bend of the trail. Then he rode back to his line.

'I'll keep the Volunteers on duty,' said Captain Joe.

'You reckon Kane's gonna pull some trick?' Campbell asked.

Malloy shook his head.

'Kane didn't count on the townsfolk turnin' out. Thought he'd ride straight through us.'

Jed was beside himself with glee.

'You thinkin' we ain't gonna see Kane agin?'

The four older men looked at him silently, their expressions grim.

'Kane'll be back,' Malloy said at last. 'An' next time he's gonna be ridin' a storm.'

CHAPTER THIRTEEN

'Malloy! Malloy!'

Campbell's shout penetrated the room at the back of the jail where Malloy had spent the night. His eyes opened immediately as the door burst open. Campbell stood framed in the doorway, his face twisted with worry.

'You gotta come quick, Malloy! Missy's out here fair set to lose her mind!'

Tension grabbed at Malloy's insides as he rolled off his bunk. He pulled on his boots, his eyes scratchy, aware that he needed more than the three hours' sleep he'd managed to snatch. Something was wrong out at Beth's place. Was this Kane making his move? He grabbed his gunbelt, securing his Peacemaker with its tie-down as he strode across the room to duck his head into the pitcher of water standing on the rough-hewn shelf. The water stung his eyes but he felt better for the short sharp shock.

He stepped into Campbell's office, rubbing his face with a scrap of cloth. Missy stood by the door, head down, her hands covering her face. She looked up through parted fingers as she became aware of his entry.

'Mr Malloy! They've taken Miss Beth! That devil has taken her away!'

The back of his neck turned ice-cold. For a moment his instinct was to cross the room and grab Missy by her shoulders. Shake some sense into Beth's black maid. Then he took a deep breath, tossed aside the cloth, and moved close to her, placing a hand gently on her shoulder.

He pulled across the chair from beside Campbell's desk and gently sat her down before dropping to one knee and easing her hands away. His face hardened as he saw down the side of her face a livid weal where she'd been struck by something.

'Tell me what happened, Missy.'

'The Lord save us all, Mr Malloy! A wagon came in the night. The man said his wife was dying and Miss Beth should come at once!' Missy took a deep snorting breath. 'I woke Miss Beth an' she got her bag and we went to the wagon. Then the devil appeared!'

'You mean Marcus Kane?'

'Yahsur, Mr Malloy. That Marcus Kane is the devil in a fine suit of clothes! He said he'd exchange Miss Beth for his brother, an' I was to tell you. Then the other man knocked me to the ground, an' I don't 'member anythin'.'

'When was this, Missy?'

'Maybe a coupla hours ago. I came as soon as I could, Mr Malloy.'

Two hours! Kane would be well on the way to the Creek by now. Malloy patted her hand.

'You've been very brave, Missy.' He thought for a moment. 'How many men with Kane?'

'Jest the one, Mr Malloy. I seen inside the wagon afore Miss Beth came out.'

'This town needs Doc Blackwell more than it needs Bart Kane,' Campbell said. 'Kane can have his brother, law or no law.'

'We're not there yet,' Malloy said grimly. 'An' Kane's playin' with fire now.'

Campbell, his face set, nodded his agreement. 'The whole town'll be agin him now. He'll be takin' her to the fort. Goddamned Kane!'

Malloy's thoughts churned around. Taking Beth was surely the last throw of the dice for a desperate man. Maybe his men had turned on him after the showdown at the edge of town. The sheriff was right. The meekest townsmen in Masonville would rise up against a man who used a woman's life as a gambling chip, especially when that woman had cared for their wives and families. But getting up a posse would waste valuable time.

He breathed in deeply. Slow down, slow down, he told himself. Maybe he was underestimating Kane. Was taking Beth merely a decoy, part of a plan to hit both the town and the big house with its Concord? For Malloy both the town and the stage came a long way after Beth but he knew he couldn't ignore them.

'Take Missy up to the big house,' he told Campbell. 'Henry and Jed to mount guard over the Concord.'

Campbell appeared to have guessed at Malloy's thinking.

'An' I'll roust out the Volunteers in case Kane's men try for Bart.'

'You got it, Sheriff! I'm gonna ride for the Creek. With Kane in a wagon I've gotta chance of catchin' them afore they reach the fort.'

Campbell shook his head.

'They're too far ahead.' His face cleared, and he held up a clenched fist in triumph. 'No! You might catch 'em, at that! Wolf Trail! Joins the main trail maybe two miles this side of the Creek.'

Malloy remembered the rarely used trail pointed out by Jed as they'd driven the wagon away from the fort. Then he realized why Bart Kane's pants had looked so wet on the day he'd surprised Malloy coming from the Peters's place. Kane and his men had swum the river, cutting off several hours from the regular trail-ride between Masonville and the Creek.

After the recent rains the river would be running high and fast. His chest tightened. If Beth was to have any chance at all he knew he had to get across that river. He became aware of Campbell's gaze.

'You OK, Malloy?'

'I'm fine. Just tell me how I get there.'

He reached behind Campbell's desk to take from the shelf a box of Winchester shells. Luckily his palomino was back of the sheriff's place instead of being at the livery. He'd need his slicker by the looks of the damp grey dawn breaking on Main Street. Hell! Were his brains becoming addled? A slicker wasn't going to keep him dry while he was crossing that goddamned river.

'Take the trail 'til you reach a coupla oaks standin' to the south. Turn north and ride maybe five miles to an arroyo,' Campbell said. 'Ride through it an' it takes you to a wide meadow. There's a burned out homestead, you'll see. Turn east after that an' you'll reach the river where it bends close to a line of birch. On the other side you'll see Wolf Trail leading through another stand of birches. Three miles on you'll join the main trail.'

Malloy nodded.

'Got it.' He patted Missy's shoulder. 'Sheriff'll take you to Henry. I'll be back with Miss Beth.'

'The Lord be with you, suh!'

Outside, on the other side of Main Street, a lamp spurted into light in one of the stores. The day was just beginning. As Malloy walked to the rear of the jailhouse he wondered if he'd see its nightfall. Unhitching the palomino's reins, he untied the morral from around the animal's head and tossed it aside, spilling its hay. He swung up into the saddle.

'Mighty glad you found your way back. I'm dependin' on you at the river,' he said aloud.

He turned the palomino's head, dug his heels into the animal's flanks and headed for the trail leading eastwards out of Masonville. Even if he had to shoot his way into the fort he was going to catch up with Marcus Kane.

This time he was going to kill the son of a bitch.

For over four hours of hard riding Malloy paced his palomino, urging the animal into a short gallop before reining into a lope for the animal to regain its wind. Then, once the animal was comfortable again, Malloy dug in his heels, spurring the animal back into a gallop. Ahead was the river crossing, but Malloy tried to push it from his mind. Beth needed him, that was all that counted now.

He turned the palomino's head as they passed the ruined homestead, its blackened timbers witness to Kane's ruthlessness.

Malloy pulled his hat lower down over his eyes as the change of direction brought him to face the wind, the palomino's pace increasing as the animal scented the water. Across the swath of land ahead of him Malloy could see the tops of trees, which he guessed were lining the riverbank.

Within fifty yards the river came into view, lower than the ground he was racing across, the stand of birches, as Campbell had described, a little way over to his right. As he closed the riverbank, the sound of rushing water came to Malloy's ears, and his chest tightened. He leaned forward to brush the palomino with his gloved hand, conscious of the sweat on the animal's neck.

They reached the trees, Malloy ducking below the branches until he was clear and then reining in within a few yards of the rushing water. The level was high, the speed of the current sweeping the water towards a wide bend in the river. As Malloy watched, figuring how he was going to cross, a log sped past, twisting and turning in the current.

Malloy cursed himself. There was no way he could have admitted to Campbell that he couldn't swim. All he'd had in his mind in the sheriff's office was that Beth needed him. If he didn't cross this river Kane would take her into the fort. There was no telling what would happen to her among that bunch of rattlesnakes.

Malloy swung down from his saddle and untied the whangs that held his slicker behind the cantle of his saddle. He unbuckled his gunbelt and wrapped it in the oilskin coat, securing the bundle again with the long buckskin strings. Then he used another whang to secure his Winchester so the leather scabbard was across the palomino's back in front of the horn.

After pushing his hat firmly down in his saddle-bag he took down his rope, dallied the end around the horn, then let out ten feet of hemp and secured it around his waist. The remaining twenty feet he held loosely in his hand. For almost a minute he stood still, his eyes on the rushing water, judging the speed of the current. Then, keeping his eye on the stump of birch on the opposite bank he walked the palomino until he was maybe thirty yards upriver.

Malloy swung back into his saddle. For a moment his hand dropped to touch the hard notch in the leather of his boot below his trail pants, and his mouth moved silently. Then he gripped his reins hard and kicked at the animal's flanks. As if charging Johnny Reb's guns Malloy let out a wild yell as the palomino hit the water chest high.

Malloy kicked his feet from the stirrups and tightened his thighs against the palomino's sides. Within seconds the horse was swimming, his head reared out of the water, his eyes rolling. The current pushed both man and horse downriver. Spray hit Malloy in the face, blinding him for a second. Goddamnit! He'd lost sight of the birch stump!

He braced his leg muscles, as he felt himself being forced from the horse's back by the strength and speed of the current. An instant later he was ten feet down-river of the palomino, held only by the hemp dallied around the horn. He sucked in air as the current pushed him below the level of the water and he kicked furiously, fear clouding his mind.

The current forced him upwards, and he broke the surface of the water, choking and spitting water from his lungs. The hemp had been snatched from his hand, and was trailed out downstream. He heaved on the line from his saddle horn, straining every muscle until the ivory-coloured tail of his horse was within inches of his grasp. His head went beneath the surface of the water and he took another mouthful of water.

His stomach heaving, he retched as he kicked himself above the surface, feeling his horse's rear leg brush against his side as the animal fought across the direction of the current. His one hand grasped the palomino's tail, then he let go of the hemp as his other hand closed over the rough hair.

'*Cuidado!*'

Malloy yelled, as though the palomino could understand the warning, as a stout log was swept in their direction. With his head and shoulders now clear of the rushing waters Malloy kicked out at the log, preventing it striking the palomino's sides. The rough bark hammered against the heel of his boot as the log was sent surging downstream.

Ahead of him the stand of birches marking the start of Wolf Trail slid past him as the current, too strong for the palomino, swept past. There were maybe twenty yards to go to the bank, and Malloy was aware that his horse was weakening. Should he attempt to grasp the long line of hemp that floated downriver? Could he slip his grasp along its length so that the current took him into the bank? As if suddenly aware of the bank, the palomino struck out more strongly. Choking water from his lungs, Malloy saw trees only ten yards away.

Then the palomino's neck rose above him, the cantle of his saddle rising as the horse touched bottom, and a moment later Malloy felt soft ground beneath his boots. He continued to grip the palomino's tail, scrabbling forward as the horse began to emerge from the water on to dry land, until at last Malloy could feel firm ground beneath his boots, and he let go the palomino's tail to stagger forward and fall on his knees.

He lay on the ground retching muddy water. After a while he climbed to his feet, sucking precious air into his lungs. Inwardly, he cursed himself for being so damned paperbacked. He'd seen young men scarcely out of britches get across rivers like that with less trouble.

Close by, his palomino had its head down nibbling at the grass, water streaming from its sides. A rueful smile showed on Malloy's face as he stepped forward to pick up his reins. Another horse and he might not have got across the river.

Then Malloy's face set hard. From his saddle-bag he dug out his hat, pulling it low over his eyes before rapidly loosening the whangs around his slicker. He buckled on his gunbelt and retied his slicker.

He slipped the whangs on his Winchester scabbard, and swung into his saddle. There was a butte close to where Wolf Trail met the main trail, he remembered. The high ground would allow him to see in both directions along the trail. There was still a chance he'd reach the butte before Kane's wagon. If luck was against him he'd follow the wagon to the fort.

'Hard ridin' again, pardner,' he said aloud,

and dug in his heels.

Half an hour later Malloy slipped from his saddle to guide the palomino up the steep slope of the butte, weaving his way between the large boulders, both man and animal scrabbling and sliding on the loose stone. Above Malloy, outlined against the sky, two large boulders offered enough cover for both him and his horse. From there, Malloy judged, the trail would be well within range of his Winchester.

By the time he reached the crest, sweat was trickling down his back beneath the woollen trail shirt. He led the palomino around the rear of the large boulder, securing his reins around the stump of a wind-blasted tree. He dragged out his brass spyglass from his saddlebag, and then unshipped his Winchester from its scabbard. Turning to the south, he scrabbled across the stone-strewn crest to look along the trail in the direction of Masonville, conscious of the light breeze against his face.

Goddamnit, he'd made it! Or had he? Maybe a couple of miles away, half-obscured by a thin dust cloud, a two-horse wagon was heading his way. Was it Kane or some decent homesteader keen to make time?

Malloy rested his long-gun on the ground

and stood up, his spyglass at his eye. Two quick turns of the eyepiece and he brought the wagon driver into focus. The man's reservation hat was clearly visible against the material of the wagon.

'You ain't got long to live, Fletcher,' Malloy said aloud.

He placed his spyglass carefully on a nearby rock and picked up his Winchester, resting it across the edge of a flat stone. The breeze wasn't strong enough at this range to affect his aim but strong enough, he reckoned, to prevent the approaching horses from scenting his palomino. Sighting along the barrel, Malloy followed the wagon's progress as it drew closer to the butte.

At the speed of the approaching wagon, he reckoned, thirty yards should be about right. A few minutes later the wagon hit the mark and Malloy fired. The slug whipped across the heads of the horses, as Malloy intended, and with a loud shout Fletcher hauled back on the reins with one hand, grabbing for the long-gun resting beside him.

As the wagon came to a halt level with the butte, Malloy levered the Winchester, brass spinning through the air. He shifted aim and fired. Fletcher slammed against the edge of the wagon and toppled over into the dirt. As Malloy sent brass spinning again into the air, ready to fire again, Fletcher twitched twice, and lay still.

Nothing moved. The sounds of gunshots drifted away, to leave only the faint trilling of a bird. Silently, Malloy gazed down. Inside the wagon were Kane and Beth. He couldn't shoot at the wagon for fear of hitting Beth. If he showed himself Kane couldn't miss at this range.

A slim arm emerged from the canvas of the wagon. He guessed Kane was forcing Beth to reach for the reins. Hesitating for only a second, Malloy put another shot into the woodwork of the wagon, hoping the horses wouldn't bolt. He'd shoot both if necessary, but that might mean the wagon going over, and Beth getting badly hurt. His muscles relaxed as the horses skittered on the dirt of the trail then settled again. The arm had disappeared back behind the canvas.

'You ain't more careful you're gonna kill your fine lady!' Marcus Kane's voice was unmistakable. 'I'm bettin' that's you up there, Malloy!'

'An' a posse!' Malloy called.

'A posse an' you'da been across the trail, Malloy!'

There was a crack of rifle fire and two feet from Malloy splinters of stone exploded into the air above his head. Malloy dropped to a crouch and rolled across the sharp stones to take cover behind another low boulder. Kane was smart. He must have been taking aim on the sound of Malloy's voice.

'You ain't used your brains on this one, Malloy,' Kane called. 'Your gal don't count for nothin'. This is between you an' me.'

Malloy glanced around. In his new position there was no way Kane could get a shot at him.

'Then let her go,' he called.

'I gotta better idea,' said Kane. 'I'll shoot her, an' then it's just the two of us.'

Malloy's grip tightened on his long-gun. Kane was ruthless enough to carry out his threat. Sure, he'd try to kill Kane after. And if he survived what would he then do with his own life? Would he carry on riding north, wear a city suit some of the time, earning his living with a gun until he got too old? Spending his nights drinking too much whiskey. Paying for company. Without Beth the job would be nothing.

Maybe meeting Beth and facing the Kanes was what he'd been heading for since that day he'd wished his brother well and ridden away from his father's land. At the fort he'd promised Beth one last present. But it was nothing when compared with Beth's life. He thought hard. Maybe there was a way both to save her and to keep his promise to Abraham Walker.

'I gotta deal for you, Kane,' he called. 'You get Bart back but there's more.'

'Keep talkin' Malloy.'

'You quit the Creek. Take your brother an' your gunnies some other place. You've made money. You get to live to spend it. Masonville gets peace and its stage line.'

There was a short pause, and then a loud bitter laugh.

'You just gonna take my word on this, Malloy?'

'No, I ain't,' Malloy called. 'You think I been punchin' beef for the past ten years? I call in favours an' less than a month you'll find an army ridin' down on you.'

For a minute there was silence. Malloy kept his eyes fixed on the wagon. Was Kane thinking about the deal, or was he planning something? Malloy studied the ground below him. He'd maybe have to find a way of getting close to the wagon if Kane didn't take the deal.

There was a sudden shout.

'OK, Malloy! How do I know Campbell will let Bart go?'

'You got my word on that, Kane!'

'OK. it's a deal. No tricks, or your woman dies.'

'Just bring her out, Kane!'

Malloy lowered his long-gun and placed it on the ground behind the rock. He drew his Peacemaker and, half-crouched, began to make his way down the steep slope, moving from rock to rock for cover. He reached even ground, his eyes never leaving the wagon, searching for any movement in the rough canvas. If a gun appeared he would be forced to shoot.

He stopped still as Beth appeared through the flap behind the driver's seat. She was gagged, a blue neckerchief tightly bound around her mouth. Her hands, Malloy saw, were tied behind her back. She was being used as a shield, blocking any shot Malloy might have been tempted to fire at the unmistakable long fine jacket topped with the Dakota hat.

Malloy, his Peacemaker down by his side, advanced warily towards the wagon his eyes fixed on the two figures as they climbed down. Malloy saw the sidearm appear briefly beyond Beth's wide skirt as she was pushed forward.

'No shootin', Kane! You got my word.'

Beth was halted some ten feet ahead of the horses. Malloy was close enough now to see Beth's eyes, wide and imploring, as she was held close, one arm around her neck.

Slowly, Malloy began to approach the pair.

'OK, Kane. You can let her...'

Beth was pushed aside. Malloy had an instant to see the sidearm emerge from behind her skirt and his Peacemaker roared. A red splash bloomed on the fine grey jacket, slamming the figure back to fall face down in the dirt of the trail.

Goddamnit! He should have known Kane would try something. Malloy holstered his Peacemaker and strode across to Beth, knife in hand. With one slash of the blade he released her hands. She tore at her gag, eyes frantic.

'Kane!' Beth screamed.

'Turn around, Malloy! Hate to shoot a man in the back!'

Slowly Malloy turned around to face the wagon. Behind the horses, looking down, stood a bare-chested Kane, wearing only rough trail pants. In his hand a Navy Colt was rock steady, aiming for Malloy. Kane nodded in the direction of the dead man on the ground.

'I guess Missy didn't know about us pickin' up Zack.'

'Thought we had a deal, Kane,' Malloy said, as he took a couple of paces to his left, moving Beth out of the line of fire.

'I changed my mind, Malloy,' Kane snickered. 'I told you once before a woman was gonna get you killed. You wanna say a prayer or anythin'?'

Malloy hurled himself headlong to his left. His Peacemaker roared and for an instant Malloy saw a red star explode between Kane's eyes, as skin and bone flew into the air. Then a hot wind slammed against Malloy's chest, blood rushed to the back of his throat, and darkness fell.

CHAPTER FOURTEEN

His thumb tucked in his gunbelt, Jed Miller looked down on the crowd of townsfolk gathered in front of the sheriff's office. The brand-new star on his shirt gleamed in the morning sunlight.

'I promise you folks I'm gonna do my best to keep this town law-abiding.' Jed grinned. 'Minding the fact that ain't gonna be too difficult now the Kanes and their gun-slingers ain't around no more.'

There were whoops and cheers from the crowd.

'Danged good job you got Henry for the writin' work,' somebody called.

Amid the laughter Henry stepped forward to stand alongside Jed.

'We're both gonna be workin' on it.' His fingers brushed the star on his shirt, teeth showing in his dark face. 'Folks, you gotta remember we're only deputies! Sheriff's gonna be mighty mad if we get things wrong.'

A huge cheer went up as Malloy stepped out of the sheriff's office, closely followed by

Beth Blackwell and Sam Stockin. In Malloy's hand was the oilskin pouch he'd taken from Strawberry Jack Wilson in the Silver Creek livery barn.

He held up the pouch.

'Some good news, folks.' He gestured to two men in the crowd. 'It's taken six months, but Cheyenne have finally confirmed the homesteaders' certificates go back to the original settlers.'

A dark-haired woman in a brown working dress gave out a little scream of joy.

'You mean, Sheriff, we can all go on home?'

'That's what it means, Emily!'

A fresh burst of cheering rang out, only halted by Malloy raising his hand.

'I'll be gone for a few weeks. First I got business in Cheyenne. Then Doc Beth tells me they have to make sure back East I'm still in one piece.'

'Next time I get shot I'm takin' Doc Beth with me!' Jed said.

Before anyone could say more, a musical blast of noise sounded at the edge of town. Galloping down Main Street came three pairs of matched horses hauling the Concord, sunlight reflected on its polished wood. Whip in one hand, six lines in the other, Cassidy sat on the box alongside Charlie

Morgan, who held a shining bugle at his lips.

As the crowd backed away, Cassidy shouted commands to the leaders as he hauled on the lines, bringing the stagecoach to a halt opposite the sheriff's office. He stood up from the box, and doffed his battered hat in the direction of Malloy.

'Walker Line stage ready for Cheyenne, Mr Malloy!'

For a moment Malloy stared wordlessly at the beaming face of the grizzled Cassidy. Since he'd been fit enough to walk, these last three months, he'd made a point of seeing the stage when Cassidy made the weekly run to Cheyenne. Each day as he'd wished the passengers a safe journey he'd thought of Abraham Walker. The major had believed the stage would be the lifeblood of Masonville. Events had proved him right.

Malloy scanned the cheerful faces of the townspeople. Many of them belonged to men and women newly arrived in town. Several of them were keen to open stores now they had confidence in the town's future. With a nod Malloy acknowledged Campbell's raised hand. The old sheriff deserved the time on his porch drinking his pappy's Scotch whisky.

Malloy raised a hand to Captain Joe and

Lucy from the bank. Both had been working with Beth these past months, preparing for her absence.

He smiled as Lucy gave him an extra wave. She knew more about him, he guessed, than lots of folk. After Beth had got him back to Masonville in the wagon, Lucy had nursed him when Beth needed to sleep. If folks ever remembered that Lucy had once been a saloon girl, they no longer thought it worth saying.

'All the bags on board?' Malloy asked Cassidy.

'Sure thing, Mr Malloy. One for Missy, couple for you, and a wagonload for Miss Beth!' He gestured towards the six horses. 'Best we got.' He pointed with his whip at the centre pair. 'Coupla new swings. Cain't have the owner behind a spike team!'

'Cassidy! You got room for Missy up there for an hour?' Henry called.

'Sure thing.'

Malloy exchanged glances with Henry, who was chuckling as he helped Missy climb up to the box. Then Malloy took Beth's arm.

'Time to go,' he said, and held out his hand to help her into the coach. Beth paused at the open door, and turned to look up at the driver.

'Cassidy! Just what is a spike team?'

Cassidy shifted the plug into his cheek and showed his tobacco-stained teeth.

'Bunch of ornery long-eared mules, Miss Beth. Cranky and slow, the lot of 'em!'

Beth, amused, took Malloy's hand and stepped up into the coach.

Malloy turned to Jed.

'You need me, you telegraph Boston.'

Miller nodded, his face serious.

'Coupla brats playin' hookey from the schoolmarm. Could be a tough deal.' Then he burst out laughing, and thrust out his hand. 'Mighty glad you came to town, John Malloy. Come back to us real soon.'

Malloy grinned. Crazy kid was never going to change. Malloy shook Jed's hand warmly, then those of Henry and Stockin. He handed the banker the oilskin pouch.

'Some extra water rights in there, Sam,' Malloy said.

Inside the coach Malloy took care to avoid stepping on Beth's skirt and settled himself opposite her. She'd taken his advice and chosen to sit with her back nearest the driver. They had a long journey ahead of them and when the Concord began to sway her seat would be the most comfortable. With a cheer from the crowd, and a blast on

Charlie's bugle, Cassidy cracked his whip above the leaders and the stage moved forward.

Through the open space of the coach door Malloy saw the townspeople waving farewell. The stores of Main Street passed by. Two boys scampered along the boardwalk, keeping pace with the walking horses. Malloy was amused to recognize the same two boys who'd witnessed his first arrival in the town. Eight months later the boys had both grown and there were gaps between their britches and woollen stockings.

The youngsters gave one last wave as the six horses were urged into a trot and Main Street was left behind. The coach began to sway as it reached the hard ground of the trail leading to the first station, where the horses would be changed. Malloy was thoughtful. The last time he'd thought of travelling this way he was set on riding north.

Malloy shifted his gaze from out of the coach as he became conscious of Beth's eyes on him.

'Sheriff Malloy of a small town,' she said. 'Some might say Pinkerton Agent Malloy sounds better.'

Malloy smiled. He knew she was teasing. Not for the first time Beth appeared to be able to read his thoughts.

'Sure they might,' he admitted. 'Famous lady surgeon sounds good, too. You gonna be hankerin' on stayin' back East?'

For a moment amusement sparkled in Beth's eyes. Then she was serious.

'I'll always want to live in Masonville.'

'An' I feel the same,' Malloy said. 'Now I'd better get started.'

Apparently ignoring Beth's startled expression, he leaned across and pulled down the leather curtains. Only the broken rays of sunshine edging around the leather curtains illuminated the interior. He crossed one leg over his knee and pulled off his boot.

'John Malloy! What are you doing?'

Wordlessly, Malloy took out a small knife and carefully made an incision inside the boot. His fingers felt the hard notch in the leather. Hiding whatever he'd found in his closed fist, he pushed his foot back into his boot, and sat back.

'Guess we ain't got space for me to go down on one knee agin. So I'll just have to show you this.'

He opened his hand. On his palm sat a gold ring. A large sapphire surrounded by tiny diamonds twinkled in the light breaking through the sides of the leather curtains.

Beth's eyes were wide, sparkling with delight.

'It's beautiful.'

'Brought by my grandmother from the Spanish court, afore she crossed the ocean and met her wild Irishman!' For a moment he hesitated, a frown etched on his face. 'Those rich folks of yourn in Boston? How they gonna feel about you getting tied to a shootist?'

Beth laughed warmly.

'You'll be a lion of society! They'll want to hear all your stories.'

Malloy shrugged his broad shoulders.

'Not much to tell.' He smiled at a thought. 'S'pose I could always speak Spanish.'

He leaned across and pulled back the leather curtain. To the east the clustered wooden buildings of Masonville were about to disappear from view around a bend. Beyond them he could see the roof of the big house upon the hill. Malloy breathed in deeply. Maybe the century hadn't left him behind, after all. Cheyenne and later Boston lay ahead of them. But he and Beth would return to Masonville. And soon.

The publishers hope that this book has given you enjoyable reading. Large Print Books are especially designed to be as easy to see and hold as possible. If you wish a complete list of our books please ask at your local library or write directly to:

Dales Large Print Books
Magna House, Long Preston,
Skipton, North Yorkshire.
BD23 4ND

This Large Print Book, for people
who cannot read normal print,
is published under the auspices of

THE ULVERSCROFT FOUNDATION